CANDLELIGHT
Supreme

"DON'T, CLINT," SHE WHISPERED AS HE SLID HIS ARMS AROUND HER WAIST AND PULLED HER AGAINST HIM.

"I still love you, Elise," he murmured next to her ear.

"But I don't love you. I stopped loving you when you deserted me at the altar and disappeared without a trace for eight months. How can you possibly expect me to care for you after that?"

As if her words had no meaning, he tightened his embrace. "It's so good to hold you again."

"Let go of me, Clint." Her voice broke, and she longed to get away from him before she lost control of her emotions. "I don't love you."

"Liar," he said simply.

117 DESERT PRINCESS,
    Hayton Monteith

118 TREASURE FOR A
    LIFETIME, *Linda Vail*

119 A DIFFERENT KIND OF
    MAN, *Barbara Andrews*

120 HIRED HUSBAND,
    Melanie Catley

121 BEYOND A DOUBT,
    Eleanor Woods

122 TORCH SONG,
    Lee Magner

123 CUPID'S DILEMMA,
    Ginger Chambers

124 A FRAGILE DECEPTION,
    Jane Atkin

125 MOONLIGHT AND MAGIC,
    Melanie Catley

126 A LOVE TO LAST
    FOREVER,
    Linda Randall Wisdom

127 HANDFUL OF DREAMS,
    Heather Graham

128 THIS NIGHT AND ALWAYS,
    Kit Daley

129 SHADOWS OF THE HEART,
    Linda Vail

130 CONTINENTAL LOVER,
    Cathie Linz

131 A MAN FOR AMY,
    Blair Cameron

132 A FORBIDDEN REFUGE,
    Eleanor Woods

TENDER BETRAYER

Terri Herrington

A CANDLELIGHT SUPREME

Published by
Dell Publishing Co., Inc.
1 Dag Hammarskjold Plaza
New York, New York 10017

Dell ® TM 681510, Dell Publishing Co., Inc.

Candlelight Supreme is a trademark
of Dell Publishing Co., Inc.

Candlelight Ecstasy Romance®, 1,203,540, is a registered trademark of Dell Publishing Co., Inc., New York, New York.

ISBN: 0-440-18557-2

Printed in the United States of America

August 1986

10 9 8 7 6 5 4 3 2 1

WFH

For Robin Kaigh—my partner, my teacher, my friend

To Our Readers:

We are pleased and excited by your overwhelmingly positive response to our Candlelight Supremes. Unlike all the other series, the Supremes are filled with more passion, adventure, and intrigue, and are obviously the stories you like best.

In months to come we will continue to publish books by many of your favorite authors as well as the very finest work from new authors of romantic fiction. As always, we are striving to present unique, absorbing love stories —the very best love has to offer.

Breathtaking and unforgettable, Supremes follow in the great romantic tradition you've come to expect *only* from Candlelight Romances.

Your suggestions and comments are always welcome. Please let us hear from you.

Sincerely,

The Editors
Candlelight Romances
1 Dag Hammarskjold Plaza
New York, New York 10017

TENDER
BETRAYER

CHAPTER ONE

The Bronco that had been riding Elise Cranston's bumper since she'd left the water experiment station was not the sole cause of her rising anger. But since it had been inappropriate to lash out at her boss when he'd broken the news just fifteen minutes ago, she figured the Bronco was as good a target for her rancor as any.

Deliberately slowing to fifteen miles an hour in a forty-mile-an-hour zone, she crept along, hoping the idiot behind her would get the message and pass her before she gave in to her instincts and slammed her brakes to make him hit her from behind. It would serve him right, she thought. But wrecking her car wouldn't solve her problems, any more than bursting into tears would. And she had neither the time nor the energy for that.

"Damn," she muttered as tremors of anxiety coursed through her. She was in no mood to do battle with a joyrider today. Yesterday, when her worst worries pertained to the lock and dam project she was working on, her patience might have served her better, but today . . .

"Get off my bumper!" Elise blared, heat scoring her features when the Bronco almost bumped her. Heavy traffic detoured around them, but the driver would not pass her. It was an omen, she thought, an omen that her refusal to look back wouldn't do the trick anymore. After what she'd learned today, she knew she'd have to look back to muster the strength to plunge forward into the inevitable. Clint Jessup was back from the black hole he'd vanished into without a trace eight months ago, and he intended to see her. The destructive driver behind her was a warning, she told herself, a warning that life was going to be a bit rougher for a while. But she had braved rough times before, and she had no doubt she could do it again.

Dreadfully anxious to be rid of the vehicle that seemed bent on driving right through her, she made a sharp turn onto a quieter street and breathed a shaky sigh of relief that she could at least drive the rest of the way in peace.

But a quick glance in the rearview mirror told her the Bronco was still behind her. Her pulse accelerated as the first light of understanding dawned on her. The Bronco was following her.

Driving fast enough to keep a car's distance between them, Elise strained to make out the driver. A man—no, two men—sat silhouetted against the sun descending at their backs. The driver's shoulders were squared with determination as he drove, and the passenger sat slumped against the door in a pose of utter boredom. An instant of panic surged through her, and her chest constricted with air that couldn't find its way out.

Making another quick turn while she held her breath, Elise watched in her mirror as the Bronco barreled around the corner after her, the sun no longer making opaque shadows out of her pursuers. The driver's hair flapped into his face from the hard wind at his window, and she watched a hand come up to push it back into place. It was dark hair, full and tapering back from his face, and against the light through his back window she could see the slightest hint of curl.

She made another turn as the panic coiling in the pit of her stomach became more pronounced. The sun was blazing toward her now, and without slowing her speed, she held up a hand to shade her eyes and glanced in the mirror again, hoping to memorize his features and report him to the police. Elise clutched the steering wheel more tightly as she waited for the bright glare to slide off the windshield and give her a clear view of his face as they rounded a curve. The open collar of the driver's shirt flapped against his neck and a ray of sunlight caught a strip of gold draping down from his throat, illuminating it like the razor edge of a knife aimed at her. Some familiar pain stabbed her heart and she released her breath in a rush. *The gold chain . . . the birthday present she had given him . . .*

"No," she said aloud before her imagination carried her away. It wasn't him. It was just the suggestion of his being back that had started her heart conjuring up images.

The sun descended behind the trees after its last blinding burst of orange, and suddenly the man came into full view through the mirror—the beckoning mane of soft, dark hair, the determined set of full lips on a tanned face, the chain glistening more subtly against his neck. And as her punctured heart sank to her stomach, her eyes rose to the dark, riveting eyes that refused to let her go—Clint Jessup's eyes.

Oh, dear God, physical danger she could bear, but Clint Jessup threatened something worse, something far worse.

Suddenly her driving became uninhibited, and her foot slammed against the accelerator. The sound and feel of metal sent a chill through her bones to rival the heat of the wound still consuming her.

As if he knew he was recognized, Clint's teeth flashed between tight lips, and he sped up as well. His shoulders hunched forward as he clutched the steering wheel, his lips moving to some inaudible cursing that she was thankful she could not hear. Searching for another turnoff in hopes of getting back into the flow and security of heavy traffic, Elise forced her eyes to stay on the road and away from the rearview mirror. But no sooner had she spotted a turnoff a mile up the deserted road than the heavy hum of his engine loomed up beside her.

Elise kept her eyes off the vehicle trying to stop her, and remained intent on reaching the turnoff that might be her salvation. But Clint had other plans. She heard his gears shift, heard the passenger in his car shouting at him, heard the squeal of his tires as he found a last burst of speed and screeched sideways in front of her. Stomping on her brakes, she steered to the shoulder of the road, skidding to a stop just short of hitting him.

The driver's door of the Bronco slammed, and in seconds Clint was at her car. Before the thought of locking her door occurred to her, he was reaching for the handle, opening it, leaning inside. Elise shoved him away and pushed out of the car, her lungs groping for air, her heart pounding. "Have you become a lunatic as well as a self-serving bastard? Are you trying to kill us?"

Clint leaned against her car door to close it. The suggestion of a smile softened his lips, and his black eyes were intimate, hungry as they swept the length of her. "Hi, Elise," he said between labored, heaving breaths.

The mildness of his greeting rankled her, but somehow she couldn't make herself get back in the car and drive away just yet. "What do you want, Clint?"

A shrug and a sigh punctuated his slowing breaths. "I just wanted to see you."

Elise slid her trembling fists into the pockets of her pants. "In the old days they used to knock on doors for that sort of thing, instead of running you down in the street."

"You would have just slammed the door in my face," Clint said. "I wanted to catch you before you got inside."

Elise turned away from his probing eyes and peered up the street, wishing she could turn back time a half hour and prepare herself for this encounter. "Next time you want to follow someone, Superman, you might be less conspicuous if you kept a few inches between bumpers."

A slow, half-smile sauntered across Clint's face, casting an angular shadow on the new, deep lines in his bronze skin. "And next time you get followed, Lois, you might avoid taking the most deserted street in the city."

Elise shrugged and went to her car, reaching past his hip to open her door. "Lesson learned. Now, if you'll excuse me."

Clint caught her shoulders and turned her to face him, his eyes narrow slashes squinting down at her. "I wanted to see you, Elise, not teach you a lesson."

Elise stepped out of his hold and assessed him guardedly, fighting back the hope that told her to give him a chance. Reason left her for a fleeting moment, her eyes softened, and she mentally brushed his hair back as it eased over his face, mentally straightened the long, thin strand of gold as it looped from his neck where she had hung it months ago, mentally traced the tapering lines of his white shirt until it disappeared behind jeans that were well-worn and faded in the most suggestive places. Slowly, her eyes dropped down the defined thighs sheathed in denim, to his calves set apart in an unwavering stance, to the threadbare jogging shoes that he had never been able to part with as easily as a lover.

16

"Why did you move out of your father's house?" he asked, his voice plaintive.

Elise glanced away long enough to tighten her tenuous grip on her unstable emotions, then brought her eyes back to his, unblinking, as if the simple movement would shatter them. "You might say I was all packed up with no place to go."

His doleful focus lowered to the pavement between them, and his throat convulsed. "I know I hurt you, running out like that before the wedding, but—"

"I survived," she cut in, desperately wanting to be spared the excuses that had taken him eight months to manufacture. She already knew the reason he had left. Nick had told her this afternoon that Clint had simply wanted to work on his book about sedimentation. *In the middle of our project?* she had flung back, unable to believe they had forgiven him for his vanishing act. But Nick had known full well what lay buried at the root of her bitterness. It was crystal clear now that Clint had come up with that flimsy excuse to conceal his cowardice for running from commitment.

"It was great to see you again, Clint," she said in a saccharine voice as she reached for her door again. "Next time you see me on the street feel free to run me off the road for a nice little chat." The door snapped open beneath her hand, but before she could step inside, Clint's fingers clamped like iron cuffs around her arm.

Though his pressure would have swung her to

17

face him, she deliberately kept her body turned toward the car. "I'm not finished with you, Elise," he said in a firm, determined voice as he stepped closer behind her and set his other hand on her stiffening shoulder.

The touch shattered her facade and exposed the raw pain hidden beneath it. She clamped her teeth shut, grating out words that cut deeper with each syllable. "What do you want from me?"

"I want you back," he said simply.

An almost hysterical laugh came from deep in her throat to thicken the air around them. Slowly, she turned to face him, carefully disengaging her arm from his grasp and narrowing her blue eyes to hide the pain lurking there. "It's about eight months too late for that, Clint. I must admit, I didn't expect you to work the freedom bug out of your system quite so soon, but—"

"It wasn't the freedom bug, Elise," Clint interrupted impatiently, his midnight eyes drawing mist to the surface of her crystalline ones. "You can't believe I wouId have skipped out on the wedding without a damn good reason."

Elise shook her head wearily and gazed off into the distance, the well of moisture in her eyes catching the light. "Clint, how should I put this? If you were kidnapped by savages and taken to some exotic island, and had to spend eight months swimming shark-infested waters to get back to me, it wouldn't make any difference. It's over. Dead. Can you understand that?"

His throat bobbed again, and he raised a finger to her chin, coaxing her face back to his in such a gentle way that she couldn't resist looking at him. "I don't believe you."

Swallowing back the emotion blocking her throat, Elise steadied her voice. "Fine, then, let's test it. *Were* you kidnapped by savages and taken to some exotic island . . . ?" As she spoke, full tears sprang to her eyes, for she hadn't realized until now how much she wished it were true.

"No," he said before she could finish. A deep, jagged breath tore from his lungs. "I can't make you understand right now. I had to get away and—"

"Write?" The word was flung as a challenge.

The lines in Clint's face seemed etched deep with regret as he looked at the ground, then glanced toward the quiet man still sitting in the Bronco, the man Elise had almost forgotten. His eyes glossed over with despair as he brought them back to her. "Yeah," he breathed out in a voice as dull as the sky in the wake of sunset.

Somehow the admission pierced her even more deeply than his disappearance had. "I'm sure the scientists of the world will appreciate the sacrifices you've made to record your incredible well of knowledge."

"Elise, don't do this," he said, sculpting her head with a touch so light that she sensed more than felt it. "I've been through hell and it's not over yet."

Elise ducked her head away from his hand and slipped into the car. "Just think how much richer your writing will be after all that suffering," she said, her voice cracking. She cranked her engine, but he leaned inside the car door, still not letting her go.

"We'll see each other at work, Elise," he said in a deep, admonishing voice. "I'm not giving up on you. You'll have to do one hell of a convincing job to make me believe that you don't care anymore."

Elise swallowed and opened her eyes, and stared at her trembling hands clutching the steering wheel as if it alone could anchor her to reality.

"I'm still crazy about you," he whispered, his hand slipping through the dark fall of her hair to settle on her neck. "An hour hasn't gone by that I haven't thought of you."

Elise knew that somewhere within her there must be some reserve of strength. But for the life of her, she could not find it. Her eyes fluttered shut, absorbing the welling beads of moisture. She opened them again as his fingers began to knead her neck. "That's very touching," she whispered without inflection. Moving her head forward, she reached for his wrist and shoved his hand away from her neck. "Now if you'll kindly move so I can shut my door . . ."

"I want to see you tonight."

"No."

"Why not?" he asked. "What are you afraid of?"

"My temper," she said.

"I know that temper. I can deal with it."

"I can't," she bit out, lips quivering. "It might land me in jail." Her face reddened to back up the words, seething blood and storming emotions threatening to implode, leaving her their only victim, if she didn't start driving.

"Then when can I see you?" The question was a pleading whisper against her face.

"I've been told I have no choice but to see you at work. But if I work it just right, that may not be very often. Now get away from my car."

Clint opened his mouth to speak again, but only a frustrated breath escaped. "I'll let you go now, but it's not over by a long shot."

Elise slipped her car into reverse. "It's your time, your energy. Waste it if you want."

Slowly, Clint stepped back and allowed her to pull her door closed. He stood watching as she backed away from the Bronco's barricade, then shifted into drive with a screech of rubber and went around it.

Numbness was something Elise would have sold her soul for at that moment, for her heart ached enormously as she glanced back at him before making her turn. He was leaning against the Bronco, elbow on the roof, a finger stroking his knitted brows as he stared after her. Quickly, she turned, leaving him behind, though the sight of him was inexorably drafted on her mind.

The car seemed to drive her home instinctively, for her thoughts were caught in the eye of her raging emotions. The anger and bitterness that she had carefully cultivated for her first meeting with him dwindled beside the bitter mingling of pain and attraction she still felt. It wasn't fair for him to come back now, she thought as she forced

21

back her menacing tears. She had just begun to get her life in order, had just become happy again after the nightmares his walking out on her had caused her.

Nightmares. She wiped at her eyes and thought how the whole eight months had been a series of nightmares. Memory settled over her like impending night as she remembered her first attempt to strike back at those nightmares . . .

"Something has happened to him!" she'd cried frantically to Gary Rivers, the police sergeant she had been involved with before Clint. It hadn't mattered that the police department had given up the "search" for Clint, deciding that they couldn't waste their time on someone who simply had "cold feet." So she had done something she'd sworn never to do. She had used her past relationship with Gary as a means to get help, despite the fact that she knew he'd never really forgiven her for choosing Clint over him.

They had spent the morning going through Clint's house in a vain search for clues. "He wouldn't have just left!" she kept saying.

Gary had rubbed his blond beard and shaken his head sorrowfully. "I'm sorry, Elise." He stepped over several boxes that Clint and Elise had packed for their move into the house they were buying, the house they had lost because Clint had been gone for the closing. "But the man knew what he was doing. He didn't leave anything really important. He took everything he'd need."

"You're not listening to me!" Her voice grated, and her eyes blared with fury. "He's hurt somewhere! Maybe dying! Maybe he's already—" The word had died in her mouth, leaving a shriveling mass where her heart had been. "If we give up on him we'll never find him. We've got to get to him!"

Gary had only shaken his head again, turning up the voltage on her fury. "We've done everything—"

"Don't say it!" she shrieked. "Don't tell me we've done everything we can. We haven't done anything! He's out there somewhere and he needs me! Why don't you believe me?"

Gary had looked at her with sympathy she could simply not bear. "Elise, it's never easy to admit that someone ran out on you. But it isn't all that uncommon for a man to get cold feet. Especially a man like Clint—"

Elise had cut off his words by grabbing him by the collar and shoving him against the wall in a burst of raging adrenaline. "He was not afraid of marriage! He wouldn't *do* that!" she had gritted. "He wouldn't leave me like that! He loves me!"

Gary hadn't said another word, and she had let him go, muttering a quiet, hoarse, "Get out. You're no help."

And she had spent the night among Clint's things, sleeping in his bed, wearing the clothes too old or too tattered for him to have taken, crying her soul out, praying that he'd walk through that door any minute and hold her.

But she hadn't seen him again.

Until today. And though she had come to terms with the ultimate rejection, she had never been able to hate him or give up on him completely, as long as the faint possibility existed that he'd left for some unavoidable reason. Not because he feared commitment. Not because he didn't love her. And certainly not so he could write.

But his reappearance today and his lack of a substantial excuse shattered those possibilities, and more than ever she had to face that the commitment had been too much for him, that *she* had not been enough.

The crunch of rocks on the driveway of her rental house pulled her out of her reverie, and mechanically, she gathered the stack of data on her seat and got out of the car. It was important to keep her routine, she told herself as she stooped to pick up the newspaper. If she just kept things normal, she would not lose control. If she kept the pain from her face, maybe she could exorcise it from her heart.

Slipping the rubber band off the paper, she used her free hand to shake it out of its roll. The front page told of the few small developments in the Givanti trial that her father's office was prosecuting. Givanti, the ex-politician who had been indicted for murder and cocaine distribution, had been almost the sole focus of the district attorney's life for the past few months, when he wasn't worrying about his daughter's emotional state. She walked out to her mailbox on the street and reached inside for the stack of mail. Her hand slipped beneath the weight, and the stack of papers anchored against her hip began to slide in a mini avalanche onto the hot May pavement. Swearing under her breath, Elise squatted and began to reconstruct the stack, glancing from side to side, hoping no one had seen the clumsy performance. The only human in sight was someone in a black Pontiac parked several houses up the street, but he seemed more engrossed in the newspaper he read than in her. *Pull yourself together,* she ordered herself. *Karen will take one look at you and see that you're falling apart.*

Pacing before the picture window off the living room, Karen watched Elise gather up her papers and mumble an expletive. Either she had already been told, she surmised, or she'd had another bad day. In either case, she'd be in a foul mood tonight. And Karen didn't blame her.

Straightening her small frame to face Elise in as positive a manner as she could to drop the bomb, she unconsciously crossed her arms over her T-shirt-covered chest and the caricature of the mosquito, which the shirt declared to be the Mississippi state bird. *No theatrics,* she told herself. *Just hit her with it straight.* Elise had to know sooner or later that Clint was back, and there was no point in dragging it out or wallowing in it.

Portentous amber eyes met tumultuous blue ones as Elise came through the door and opened her mouth in somber greeting. "Before you say anything, sit down," Karen ordered, stemming her hello with an outstretched hand. "Your father called with some news that is probably going to shake you up."

Elise shrugged out of her blue lab coat and tossed it onto the couch. "Unless I already know it."

Karen wasn't convinced. "What is it you think you know?"

Her friend's caution almost made Elise smile. "I know Clint's back."

Crestfallen, Karen let her shoulders sag. "Oh. How did you know?"

"He ran me off the road a few minutes ago."

"Ran you off the road? Are you hurt?"

Not physically, she wanted to say, but instead she shook her head and slumped onto the couch. "How did Dad know?"

Karen lowered to the coffee table across from her. "He said Clint had come to see him today. Apparently he just got back into town this morning and was intent on finding you. What did he say?"

Elise swallowed. "What difference does it make? I told him that I don't want to see him again."

"Did he say why he left?"

Elise felt the life draining from her face, leaving behind a hollow, expressionless shell. "He had to write a book about sedimentation."

"What the heck is that?"

"It's the way matter settles in the bottom of liquid. In a river, it can cause a lot of problems with ships and barges passing through."

26

"And he left you to write about *that?*"

Elise shrugged with feigned insouciance. "That's his story, anyway."

Silence provided the response that Elise expected. Karen propped her elbows on her bare knees and smoothed her short, tawny hair behind her ears. After a long while, the young woman's voice came, quiet and uninflected. "I guess I really expected there to be more."

"Yeah. Guess I did too." The admission made Elise's voice catch, and to avoid seeing the uncharacteristic wave of sympathy washing across Karen's face, she stood up and went into the kitchen. "What's to eat? I've got a ton of work to do tonight. I have to review all this data and try to figure out where to put the dikes to correct the problems we're having."

"Anything I can do?" Karen asked. She followed Elise and leaned against the kitchen doorjamb. "Like listen?"

Elise's hands fell limp on the package of sandwich meat she had reached into the refrigerator for. "Thanks, Karen. I just don't want to talk about it right now."

Karen slid up onto the kitchen table, for she rarely used chairs. "Good. At least you're not going to pretend it doesn't bother you."

Elise abandoned the meat and closed the refrigerator door, letting her eyes rest on her hands gripped around the handle. "Yes, I am. As soon as I get over the shock, I plan to do just that."

"But not to me."

Elise crossed her arms and leaned back against

27

the refrigerator door. "No, not to you. I've always been pretty transparent to you."

"And to Clint."

Elise lifted her brows doubtfully. "Yeah. But if I was transparent today, he saw a whole barrage of conflicting signals, because I don't even know how I feel about seeing him or working with him again."

"Working with him?" Karen's back straightened. "Wait a minute. They're letting him come back?"

Elise nodded. "All I can figure is that he knows where Nick's bodies are buried. Last week that guy fired a technician without batting an eye because he'd been sick too much with his allergies, and they've been laying people off left and right. But Clint Jessup drifts back into town and they bow at his feet."

"Amazing," Karen mumbled, crossing her feet in front of her.

Elise pulled out a chair and sat on one foot, combing a hand through her hair and trying not to renew her fury of the afternoon. "Nick said Clint is one of the most respected engineers we've ever employed, and that occasionally one has to overlook small lapses in judgment. He said the corps of engineers couldn't afford to reject a man of Clint's experience and intelligence. Can you believe that?"

"So you'll see him every day," Karen said grimly.

"No, I won't," Elise said. "If Nick's smart, he'll put Clint on one of the other projects. Since

28

he's coming in in the middle, anyway, it shouldn't make any difference at all."

"But you'll still see him, regardless."

Elise's shoulders sagged and she cradled her forehead in her hand and whispered a soft moan. "What am I going to do?"

Karen, who didn't believe in fostering self-pity, slid off the table and disappeared into the living room, then returned with Elise's load of data. Dropping them down with a thud on the kitchen table, she set her hands on her hips. "You're going to go on with life as if he never came back. You're going to bury yourself in your work until the shock wears off, and then you'll be fine. Better than fine."

The wisp of a smile softened Elise's face, and she pulled the papers in front of her. "My kingdom for a bag of pistachios," she mumbled.

"I just bought a whole bag," Karen said triumphantly, pulling a bag of Elise's "nerve food" out of the cabinet. "I had a feeling you might need them today."

"Bless you," Elise said as a genuine smile crept across her face. Her heart lightened at her friend's easy approach to life's catastrophes. But as she cracked open the first pink shell, she realized she was kidding herself if she thought the problem of Clint Jessup could be solved with a pat on the back, a stack of work, and a few hundred pistachios.

CHAPTER TWO

If only I could explain, Clint thought dismally as he stepped into the shelter housing the scale model of the portion of the Red River where Lock and Dam Number 3 would be placed. But he knew better than to try to explain. It was too early. In a few days it might all be over, and then . . .

Clint caught his breath as his eyes adjusted to the dark interior of the aluminum shelter, and he saw Elise standing with her back to him, staring down with unseeing eyes at the mock concrete river flowing at her feet. She was thinking about him, he thought. He felt it as strongly as he felt that she still loved him, but the knowledge was not enough for him until he could convince her to surrender to her feelings.

Eight months without her, he thought with a shudder. Eight lonely, impatient months, wishing to God that one miserable night that changed his fate had never taken place. Eight months praying that someone else would not come along to replace him, that she would wait . . .

He watched her sweep her hair back from her face and hold it above her head, then let it fall in a helpless tumble around her shoulders. Her heavy sigh moved her shoulders, and she dropped her head and rubbed her eyes. She was as tired as he was, he thought. The months had taxed her spirit too. He wondered how many months it would take to get it back in either of them.

He had almost made her his wife, he mourned, and the scars in his heart hurt him anew. He had almost had the chance to begin a life with her. Instead, he found himself without her smile for longer than he'd ever expected, and now he was reduced to staying out of sight and watching her from afar, with the awestricken feelings of apprehension that he'd known when he'd first fallen in love with her. It had been a constant struggle to keep from reaching out and pulling her into his arms when she had worked beside him as his co-op student while she worked on her engineering degree at Mississippi State University. He had argued frequently with the voice inside him that warned him not to get involved with a woman who was so young and had been placed under his direction, especially when she was seeing someone else. But when she had graduated and he learned that she had ended her previous relationship with Gary Rivers, he felt the obstacles lifting, and he had lost the struggle with his heart . . .

It was the night of the graduation party that some of the engineers and technicians had thrown for the two co-op students who had worked with them in the hydraulics lab. Elise had been one of them, and he still remembered the coy, direct looks she'd given him through the laughing faces, the bright blue twinkle of her eyes as she sipped her drink, the way her blue satin blouse had revealed her lovely cleavage. He'd known his interest was dreadfully obvious to everyone, but it didn't seem to matter. All that mattered was the need to hold her in his arms, to breathe the scent of silky hair that had flirted mercilessly with his senses, to feel the smooth texture of her neck against lips aching for her taste . . .

He approached her, his dark, smoky eyes smiling forebodingly, and she stood up to face him with a perceptive, so-what-do-you-want-to-do-about-it lift of her delicate chin. "So, you're a full-fledged engineer now," he said.

One corner of Elise's full lips tipped upward, and she answered, "We're equals now."

"Are we?" he asked softly. Was she making conversation, he agonized, or was she offering him a hint that the time had come? His grin betrayed his interpretation. "What do you think we should do about that?"

"It all depends," she said. Were her eyes twinkling with anticipation, or was that their natural state? He honestly couldn't remember.

"On what?" Unconsciously, his hand came up to push her thick, lustrous hair back. It lingered on the silky strand against her satiny skin, and he felt her cheek grow hot.

"On how you see me. Am I some kid you've developed a friendly attachment for . . . or am I . . . ?" Her voice trailed off, as if the rest of the bold question embarrassed her.

He could feel the smile draining from his face. Thank God, they *were* talking about the same thing. "Definitely not a kid," he whispered, cupping her chin and stroking her bottom lip with his thumb. "And this attachment I have for you goes miles beyond friendly."

He felt her lip trembling beneath his touch, and she swallowed.

"What then?"

He slanted his head, and moved a fraction closer. "Elise Cranston, I see you as a maddeningly attractive woman, and I will die a miserable, premature death if I don't kiss you right this minute."

Her lips curled in the beginnings of a smile. "Then what are you waiting for?" she asked.

"For you to say that it doesn't matter that we're surrounded by forty people who will see me kiss you. Because I don't want to wait."

"It doesn't matter," she whispered.

He had always counted himself a strong man, a man who wasn't easily moved, a man who kept his head. But the moment their lips met and he was holding her in his arms, he knew he was irrevocably lost.

Her kiss consumed him completely, bringing his body to wild, fierce life, making his hands ache for free passage to the curves and lines of her body. She touched his face with hands soft

33

enough to melt the coldest heart, and he surrendered to the fact that he would never let her go.

No other woman had ever made his heart burst with triumph. No other woman had ever made him want the moment to drag into eternity. No other woman had ever made him love so deeply that he would have sold his soul to hold her for five more minutes . . .

And there had not been another woman since that night. He had loved her mind, her beauty, her generosity, and her loving ability to give. His absence had only made those feelings stronger. No, he thought, as he started toward her in the dark shelter, knowing she didn't hear his footsteps across the foot-high catwalks because of the resounding noise of the engines that made the mock river flow. For him, there would never be another woman.

Had he left her for another woman? Elise thought as she stared, unfocused, at the coal, meant to simulate sediment on a smaller scale, as it settled to the bottom of the water. Had it been some asinine, male desire that had wrenched him away? Hadn't the love she'd believed in been a little too good to be true?

An hour hasn't gone by that I haven't thought of you. His words echoed in her mind. *Then why?* she wanted to cry out. *Why did you do that to us?*

As if in answer, she heard the rattle of footsteps on the catwalks bridging the "river," and knowing her co-workers were on their lunch breaks, she closed her eyes. Somehow, she sensed his presence before his warmth enveloped her. A familiar scent drifted to her nostrils, and she stiffened as the roughened fingers of a masculine hand closed gently around her arm. "I'm sorry, Elise," Clint said in a tone that was more breath than voice.

The touch was too potent, and Elise could not trust herself to turn and face him. A tear seeped into her lashes, but she kept her eyes closed.

Clint lowered his mouth to her hair, kissed it, then laid his forehead there. She felt his chest brush against her back, felt his hard thighs graze her legs, felt the fusion of their hearts telling her that she had a dreadful fight on her hands if she intended to forget him.

"Don't, Clint," she whispered, but in answer he slid his arms around her waist and pulled her back against him.

"I still love you, Elise," he whispered next to her ear.

Why couldn't she hate him? Why couldn't she summon enough anger to push him away and convince him that there was no feeling? "But I don't love you."

As if her words had no meaning, he tightened his embrace. "It's so good to hold you again," he murmured against her neck.

"Let go of me, Clint." Her voice broke as she spoke, and she longed to extract herself from his embrace before her brimming emotions burst forth. Pinching the bridge of her nose, she said it again, more firmly, "Let go of me."

Clint turned her to face him, forcing her to look up into his pleading eyes. "Look me in the eye and tell me you don't love me," he challenged. "Your eyes don't lie. They never have."

Elise's cheeks stung with heat. "This is not a game, Clint. I'm not going to tolerate this kind of scene every time our paths cross."

"Look me in the eye and say it," he repeated.

A moment of silence rippled between them, as Elise looked up into his opaque black eyes and summoned all the strength she contained. "I don't love you anymore."

Clint's narrowed eyes bored into hers, searching, finding, measuring. "I still don't believe you."

"Fine, then," she said, her face burning. "Delude yourself. I don't care what you think." Trembling, she raised a hand to sweep back her hair, and Clint caught it. He regarded her fingertips, stained pink from the dozens of pistachios she had cracked open during the night to calm her frazzled nerves, and he brought eyes that twinkled victoriously back to hers.

"Pistachios? Something bothering you, Elise?"

Elise closed her hand into a fist and stepped backward. "All right, Clint. I'll admit it shook me up a little to have you come back to town so suddenly, and I'm aggravated at Nick for letting you have your job back. It has to do with anger, Clint, and resentment. Nothing else."

Clint stepped toward her and coaxed her fingers out of their curl, stroking them open. "There are blisters here, Elise," he said softly. Slowly, he

36

brought her fingers to his mouth, closed his lips over them one at a time, and sucked the salty taste while his eyes impaled her. Elise swallowed and gazed up at him, mesmerized, as her frayed nerve endings made her as fragmented and sensitized as the first time he had touched her.

"Stop it, Clint," she choked without conviction, knowing her fingers trembled treacherously against his lips.

"I can't," he whispered.

Wearily, she pulled her hand away, and tucked it behind her back. "Play your games on someone else. I'm all used up."

"I know the feeling," he said, finally allowing her the distance she so desperately needed. "But blisters heal, Elise. I can make it up to you."

"No, you can't. Not when it was so easy for you to waltz out and waltz back in. Everything's always been easy for you, hasn't it? Well, not this time. It'll be a cold day in hell before I ever trust you again."

He reached for her again, but Elise recoiled, stepping back onto a poorly supported catwalk covering a dry "river" model. The structure tumbled a twelve-inch distance to the ground with the resounding crash of an entire structure, and Clint caught her before she fell with it. Suddenly, a man bolted through the double doors of the shelter, hand poised under his nylon Windbreaker.

"It's okay," Clint yelled quickly to the man, stopping him with a raised hand. "It was the catwalk."

The man assessed the situation briefly, flashed Elise an innocent, composed smile, then sauntered away as if going for a summer stroll.

Forgetting the collapsed catwalk and the rush of emotion that caused her to fall, Elise balanced herself and brought distrustful eyes back to Clint. "Is that the man who was with you in the Bronco yesterday?"

Clint stooped down and began to straighten the catwalk. "Sam's a friend of mine. Want an introduction?"

Elise wasn't satisfied. "What is he doing here? Why did he come running like that?"

"He's funny that way," Clint evaded. He stood up, and she noted the deep lines running like fissures between his eyebrows, lines that hadn't been there months ago. He brushed his hands off, and set them on his hips. "Do you want to meet him or not?"

"I don't need to acquaint myself with your new friends, thank you. Now, if you'll excuse me, I think I'm going to take the rest of the day off." She made her way across the narrow catwalk and started toward the exit.

Clint followed. "You can't take a day off just like that."

"Why not?" she volleyed. "You took eight months off just like that. At least I'm using sick leave. It's a valid excuse, since I've got a monstrous headache and a pain in the neck that refuses to leave me alone."

"But Elise—"

"Stick around, Clint," she said as she hurried

away. "In a minute there should be plenty of people around for you to badger. We've even got a new co-op student you can conquer. You don't need me." And before he could detain her again, she was out the door, hurrying across the reservation as if her sanity depended on it.

For she was certain it did.

Elise lay on her stomach on the chaise longue, letting the sun pour down on her back. Her face was buried in her arms, effectively hiding the torment that she'd held in check since she'd left the shelter. It had been too much for her to go home and continue feigning composure for the benefit of Karen, who popped in and out of the house all day long. So she had come here, to her father's house, knowing he was in court. Donning the swimsuit she kept in her old room, she had found sanctuary beside the pool, hoping the sun's heat could act as a sedative to calm her heart.

If she could have cried, some of the soul-deep sadness might have been relieved, but her eyes were as dry as barren craters in godforsaken earth. Her despair found new levels, even beneath the agony that Clint's leaving had caused. What disturbed her now was that Clint had betrayed her in such a cyclopean way, then thought he could erase it all with a simple touch and some whispered words of regret.

The unfeelingness of it all ripped at her, leaving scars that she hoped would remind her the next time she was weak. She realized now that it had been weakness to delude herself while he was gone. New misery welled up as she remembered the letters she had written to him at first, a form of therapy that had helped her to cope. She had spilled her heart out in them, knowing he would never see them. And whether they had been packed with curses or lamentations, they had all ended with, *Clint, where are you, where are you, where are you?*

And today he could walk up behind her at work, slide his arms around her, and expect her to accept him as if the months of loneliness and humiliation had never occurred. Those presumptions hurt her almost as much as his leaving had.

A door closed at the house, and Elise snapped her head up to see her father coming toward her. She gave a quick wave, pulled up off the chaise longue, and dove into the pool as if the cool water could wash the expression from her face. Rich sable hair turned to a long, sleek cap as she split the surface of the water. "Feels great, Dad. Come on in."

"I didn't know you were coming by today," the stern-looking district attorney said, although his handsome gray eyes twinkled with pleasure at the unexpected sight of his daughter. "Why aren't you at work?"

"I had a headache so I took off," she said. "I thought you were in court."

"We've recessed until this afternoon, so I came home for some peace and quiet. The media will probably be banging on the door any minute now."

Elise pulled out of the pool, reaching for the

towel and drying off her face, where she hoped she wore a more pleasant expression. "If you were going to get so involved in this case, why didn't you handle it yourself instead of giving it to an assistant?"

Cranston squinted in the sunlight and shrugged. "Breard deserved it. He wanted it. He'll probably be behind my desk in a few years, anyway."

The logic seemed misplaced somehow, but Elise wrote it off to her father's fatigue. "So how's it going?"

"Slow," her father said, running a hand along his gray temples. "Givanti's a weasel who had so many gambling debts that he started distributing cocaine to pay them off. Has mush for brains. It's a wonder he ever held office in this state. Unfortunately, though, he has a shrewd attorney."

"But you're shrewder, right?" Elise said with a smile.

"That's what they tell me." He sat down on the lounge chair next to hers, and clasped his hands between his knees. "So, how are things with you?" A look of concern gilded his silver eyes. "You looked a little upset when I came out."

That sympathetic look and tone were the very things that had prompted Elise into moving away from the huge estate after Clint left, for though she knew her father loved her dearly and suffered with her, she couldn't bear the constant reminders of what had happened. Karen's no-nonsense approach to heartbreak had been exactly what

41

she'd needed. "I'm fine, Dad. Don't worry about me."

As if knowing when to quit after months of dealing with her hot-and-cold moods, Eric Cranston stood up and smiled. "Well, I'd better go fix myself a sandwich. Want one?"

The knots in Elise's stomach had left her appetite dead to anything except pistachios. "No thanks."

The man shrugged. "All right. Maybe another time." As if he couldn't think of anything else to say, he slid his hands into his pockets and started back toward the house. "Oh, by the way," he said as an afterthought, turning around. "Did you by any chance notice that black sedan parked in front of the Millers' house when you drove up?"

"No, why?" Elise had been in such an emotionally explosive state when she'd come here today that a submarine could have been parked in front of their neighbors' house and she wouldn't have noticed.

A deep frown clefted his forehead, and he rubbed his jaw. "Just wondered. This trial has me paranoid. He's probably just waiting for the Millers to get home."

"Must be," Elise said, wrapping her towel around her as a breeze made her shiver. "It wasn't Clint, was it?"

As if the question warranted his full attention now that she had broached the subject, her father came back to her. "No, not Clint. I suppose you've seen him by now, huh?"

Elise brought the towel up to her hair to hide her haunted expression, and she nodded.

Her father turned to the blue water, and focused on the sunlight reflecting from the surface. "Thought so. He seemed pretty intent on starting things up again when he was here yesterday."

Elise dropped the towel to her lap, and looked at the multicolored stripes. "He thinks I should just forgive him and run back into his arms."

Her father's unusual momentary silence was more eloquent than his words. "There are worse things you could do."

Elise regarded her father's back, set stiff with apprehension at her inevitable rebuttal. "What did you say?"

Eric turned toward his daughter, his eyes tilted in an apologetic arch. "I just want to see you happy again, honey."

Elise couldn't believe what she was hearing. "And you think I could be happy with a man who ran out on me? A man who humiliated me by practically leaving me at the altar? Have *you* forgiven him?"

"He isn't asking for *my* forgiveness," her father said in a wooden voice.

"Well, call me unreasonable," Elise clipped, jerking the towel back up and stretching it around her shoulders. "But if Clint Jessup wants forgiveness he'd better take it from anyone who offers it, because he won't get it from me!"

Her father's shoulders descended with his heavy expulsion of breath. "I didn't mean to get you all—"

"I'm fine," Elise said. She got up and started toward the house. "I'm going back to work. I don't have time to worry about Clint Jessup anymore. It seems he has enough sympathetic people to do that already." She looked back as she reached the door, saw the look of pity on her father's face, and cursed Clint Jessup all the more for being the one who put it there.

CHAPTER THREE

Dad's paranoia is contagious, Elise thought, glancing quickly over her shoulder. She almost expected to see someone sneaking between the cars behind her as she hurried to the hydraulics lab to talk to Nick about putting Clint on a different project. Halfway back to work, she had noticed that the black car her father had described was tailing her.

Coincidence, she told herself without conviction. There must be hundreds of black sedans in Vicksburg, and her imagination was making more of it than there was.

Nick wasn't in his office, so she stepped inside to his window and peered out toward the parking lot. When nothing unusual caught her eye, she breathed out a long, shaky breath and set her bag on Nick's desk. "You're getting jumpy, Elise," she mumbled aloud. Clint Jessup's sudden return had distracted her in more ways than one. Stepping back, she glanced up the street to her right, and her stomach lurched at the sight of the waiting black Pontiac. Threading her fingers through her hair, she expelled a low, dreadful moan and realized the driver was waiting for her.

"What is it?"

The sound of Clint's voice made her swing around, and she caught her breath in a ragged gasp. "Don't you have anything better to do than just hang around here when you're not even back on the payroll yet?"

Clint ignored the question and glanced past her out the window. "What were you looking at?"

Elise set her hand on her chest as if it could calm her constricted lungs, and turned back to the window, fighting the rebellious urge to tell him it was none of his business. She was becoming frightened, and he was the only one there at the moment. "It's just . . . that car. It's been following me."

Without questioning her suspicion, Clint stepped into the office and squinted up the street at the car she pointed to. When he saw it, his eyes closed and a long, tangled breath wound out of his lungs. "How long has this been going on?" he asked.

She didn't answer at first, because she wasn't sure.

"How long?" he asked more urgently.

"I don't know," she said. "I think he might have followed me to my dad's house today. I may have seen the car yesterday, too, but I can't say for sure."

"Damn!" The word came out as a craggy whisper. Clint took Elise by the shoulders and turned her to face him. She felt a slight shiver in

his hands, saw genuine fear and haunted despair in his eyes. "Listen to me, Elise," he said, his hoarseness contradicting his steady monotone. "I have to go get Sam. He's right down the hall. I'll be right back, and I'll take you home. Don't leave here until I get back. Do you understand me?"

"But . . . I'm waiting for Nick."

"Forget Nick," he insisted. "Just give me your car keys."

"My keys?" The keys were at the top of her bag, and reluctantly, she surrendered them. "What are you—?"

"No questions now, Elise. Just wait right here. Please."

Frightened at the adamant, admonishing look in his eyes, Elise nodded acquiescence. She stood frozen, listening to the squeak of his rubber soles as he ran up the corridor, heard the exchange of muffled voices, heard Clint's athletic breathing as he ran back to her office. When he got there, he closed the door and leaned over her desk to catch his breath. "I'll drive you home, Elise. And I want you to promise me that you won't go anywhere alone. Nowhere."

"Clint, you're scaring me."

"Good," he said. "Then maybe you'll listen to me. Come on." He straightened, reached for her arm, but she stepped back.

"Clint, I need to talk to Nick."

"To hell with Nick, Elise!" he rasped. "There's something more important at stake here. Now come on! And keep quiet."

Elise suppressed her rising sense of panic as

Clint reached for two white hard hats and handed one to her. "Stuff your hair up in this and pull it low over your face."

Nervously, she obeyed, then followed him down the dim corridor. She felt his hand trembling as it looped around her waist, heard the heavy, rhythmic sound of his breath, tasted apprehension rising like a lethal flood to drown her senses. Before they were out of the building, he stopped and pulled a pair of mirrored sunglasses out of his pocket, put them on, and set his hard hat on his head. "Now, walk fast," he told her. "And don't say anything until we're on our way."

She nodded and swallowed the fear flooding her throat, and took temporary refuge in his arm as it wrapped protectively around her. They walked at a fast gait to the Bronco, and he let her in his side and slid in next to her. The engine rumbled to life, and Clint backed out of his space.

Five minutes had passed before Elise found her voice. "Clint, you know you've just scared ten years off my life, don't you?"

Clint glanced in the rearview mirror, then set his hand on her knee and gave a slight squeeze. "I'm sorry, babe. I didn't think this would happen."

"You've got to tell me what's going on."

Clint only stared at the road ahead, swallowed, and glanced in the mirror again. In a voice racked with frustrated despair, he said, "I don't even know where you live now."

Breathing out a shuddering sigh at his evasion

of her question, Elise gave him her address on a street he was familiar with, then tried again. "Clint, are you in some kind of trouble?"

Clint removed his hand from her knee and brought it back to the steering wheel. "First, let me get you home, Elise."

"Then you'll answer my questions?"

"Then you can ask them," he said.

Several more explosively silent moments passed as Clint wove through the streets leading to Elise's house. "I'm going to park in that shopping center a couple of blocks behind your street. Do you have a back door?"

A cold, nauseous feeling began to take hold of her, and Elise glanced through the back window. "Why do I have the feeling that any minute now a SWAT team is going to surround us and start shooting?"

Clint only swallowed. "Do you have a back door or not?"

"Oh God, yes, I have a back door," she whispered.

"Then we'll have to come up through your backyard and go in that way so we won't be seen."

Anger sprouted where fear had taken root. "Clint, people see me going in and out of my house all the time and nothing's ever happened before."

"Things have changed, Elise," he said, his lips growing taut across his teeth.

"Why?"

The heel of his hand landed violently on the

49

steering wheel. "Because I came back to town, damn it!"

The Bronco whipped into the crowded parking lot at the shopping center, and threaded through the spaces until it stopped. But Elise didn't care where they were, for her eyes were set on Clint, seeing the haze of truth for the first time since he'd come back. She had wished there were some deeper explanation for his leaving her, and now there was. Oh, God, there was. And she wasn't sure she wanted to know it, after all.

When the engine was dead, Clint cupped her chin and gazed into her eyes. Through his mirrored glasses she saw only herself, blurry blue eyes full of fear and turmoil, a face growing paler by the moment, full lips trembling at what was becoming obvious. "If I'd had any idea . . ." he began, but then he just shook his head helplessly and opened the door. "Come on. Take the hat off and we'll get you home."

They crossed streets like lovers on a stroll, stole through yards like prowlers in the night, and approached her back door like escaped convicts waiting to be caught. "Where are my keys?" she whispered when they reached the house.

"I gave them to—That was your house key too?" His impatient voice was rising in pitch.

"Don't worry," Elise said, quelling his outburst with a trembling hand. "I have one here under the mat."

"Under the mat?" he whispered accusingly.

Ignoring his tone, Elise opened the door and they slipped inside. Clint closed and locked it behind them, his eyes bright with disbelief. "You actually keep a key under your mat where any fool could find it?"

"It's a good thing, under the circumstances," Elise volleyed. "Considering you handed my keys over to some stranger."

"Sam is not a stranger," Clint said, taking off his glasses and bolting through the house to peer through the curtains.

"Then who is he?"

"A good friend."

"Is he in trouble too?" Her voice shook as she posed the question, and Clint turned from the window.

A hand mussed his hair distractedly. "Elise, I wish I could explain this to you."

Elise lowered to her sofa, her backbone rigid. "So do I. You do intend to, don't you?"

Clint fell back next to her on the sofa, covered his face with both hands, slid them wearily down until he peered at the wall over his fingertips. "No. No, I don't."

Elise couldn't believe what she'd heard. "Do you mean to tell me that you've just scared me half to death and you don't think I deserve an explanation?"

Clint folded his sunglasses and put them in his pocket. His eyes sparkled with pain that went levels beyond what she had seen in them before. "You deserve one, Elise. But I can't give it to you."

"*Can't?*" she repeated, aghast.

"It's for your own good," he said.

51

Fire danced in her glowering eyes, and she sprang off the couch. "My own good? Was your leaving eight months ago for my own good? Was it for my own good that you popped back into town yesterday, just when my life was going well again? Is it for my own good that you've managed to make me afraid to walk outside my door?"

His unfathomable eyes held her with an embrace that reached right to her soul. "Yes," he said.

Elise brought a hand to her forehead, beginning to ache with tension and clearer understanding. "I can't believe this. You've done something illegal, haven't you?"

Clint's face was a portrait of regret. He took her hands and pulled her back down beside him, held her shoulders, pressed his forehead against hers. Heavy breaths punctuated his rising emotions. "I should never have come back."

"But you did!" Elise cried, setting her hands on his chest where she could feel life pulsating against her. "And now I have to go on working with you and seeing you all the time, pretending that things are fine when I don't know who you are or what you're involved in anymore."

"You won't have to work with me. Obviously I can't go back to work now."

"Obviously?" Elise choked out. *"Is* it obvious?"

Clint slid his hands up through her hair, encasing her head in splayed fingers as he tipped her face to his. "I'm so sorry, Elise. So sorry."

Elise felt her resolve and anger slip as his lips

hovered over hers for a desperate fragment of eternity, his eyes moving from her hair to lips wet with fresh tears, to the movement of her throat. Their eyes fused before their mouths, and forgiveness was an involuntary element that glistened from her depths. The inches separating their faces narrowed, and when his lips touched hers, she could feel the shivering tension of restrained passion.

Their tongues came together in brazen reunion as her hands molded to his narrow waist, glided over the muscles spanning his ribs, pressed against the heaving planes of his chest. Through his shirt she could feel his heart pounding in furious rhythm with her own. His clean, exotic scent drew her fingers to the soft spot of his neck just below his jaw, across the stubble of his chin, and into the hair that was just as soft as she remembered. She savored the feel of it, etching it tragically on her memory, as if it would be her last one of him.

His lips left hers and glided across her face until his tongue feathered the small shell of her ear, his breath a rhythmic whisper sending shivers down her spine. His arms held her tighter against him as his lips touched her throat. She closed her eyes as a shiver of despair coursed through her. *God help me,* she thought. His arms felt like home, and that was something she'd been without since he'd left.

But along with the love struggling out of its dormancy was fear of the unknown. For Clint had changed, had become a hunted animal who could disappear again without a moment's notice, leaving her drained, broken, and alone for the second time.

Unable to endure another moment of the madness consuming her, Elise shook free of him and slid back, fighting the desire impelling her back into his arms. "What am I supposed to do, Clint? Just accept what you tell me without asking questions? Why did you even come back?"

"I thought it was okay to come back," he said, leaning toward her. "I wanted to see you again, make it up to you."

"And you didn't count on the cops noticing?"

"Elise, I needed you—" He reached out with the words, but Elise shook his hands off of her and stood up.

"And I needed you! Eight months ago when our wedding was planned! I needed you all those nights that I cried myself to sleep, pretending you were somewhere thinking of me, trying to get back to me—"

"I was."

"Like hell you were. You were off running from the law for doing God-only-knows what! I only wish I knew what our life together was worth to you. What did you trade it for, Clint?"

A muscle in Clint's forehead twitched. "You're wrong, Elise. It wasn't that way at all."

"Why should I believe you?"

"Because you know me better than anyone else ever has."

"I don't know you at all! The Clint I knew didn't commit crimes. He didn't run from his mistakes. He wouldn't have vanished off the face of the earth a week before his wedding."

"I'm the same man I've always been," Clint said wearily.

"Then I have a terrific flaw in judgment!" Elise railed, her face burning with rage. A few moments went by, and Clint stood before her, shoulders heaving with restrained emotion, hands hanging at his sides, as if he desperately wanted to touch her but wouldn't allow himself to again.

The spitting roar of Karen's Volkswagen Bug seemed to shake the house as it pulled into the driveway.

"Is that Karen?" Clint asked, breaking the silence.

Elise nodded.

"Then I'll go," he said quietly. "I want you to promise me that you'll do your best not to be alone. Even if it means going to work with Karen."

Elise looked at the ceiling as her troubled eyes finally filled with unshed tears, and she dropped onto the couch. When Clint squatted in front of her, she looked down at him. "Are you really not coming back to work?" she asked, nostrils flaring with restraint.

"No," he whispered.

"You're going to disappear again, aren't you?" Her voice was so shaky that she could barely get out the words.

"I don't know," he said.

"Are . . . are you really in that much danger?"

Clint only closed his eyes, but the answer was clear.

Elise choked back a sob when he finally stood up to leave, and she rose to face him, fighting the urge to throw her arms around him and beg him to tell her that when he left he would be safe, that she would see him again. But deep in her heart she knew it was not true.

"So," she said in a hoarse voice as she wrapped her arms around her own waist instead. The rest of the superficial words seemed to get clogged in her throat.

"So," he said, as if he, too, struggled for an appropriate departing line, but came up empty. His eyes were black shadows full of mystery and despair, shadows in which she was captured against her will. "I hope you'll forgive me for screwing up your life."

Elise forced out a dry laugh that was negated by the tears still clouding her eyes. "No problem," she said with gentle sarcasm.

The front door opened, and Karen, engrossed in the mail, didn't see them as she stepped inside. When she set her purse down and glanced up, she crossed her arms and nodded as if the sight of Clint didn't surprise her. "Well, well," she said. "The prodigal fiancé returns." Glancing back at the mail, she began to open an envelope.

Clint's eyes remained fused with Elise's. "It's nice to see you too, Karen."

Karen cocked a perfectly arched brow and gave Elise a questioning look.

But Elise still stared at Clint, as if he would dissolve before her very eyes.

"Someone'll get your car back to you soon," he said.

Their eyes clung in an embrace that they couldn't bear to let go. The tension kept them from noticing when Karen pulled the page out of the envelope. "What the devil?" she muttered, again not penetrating their fulminating thoughts. But her startled, "Wait a minute. Is this some kind of threat?" dragged both pairs of eyes to the letter.

Elise took the paper and saw clipped magazine letters glued to the page. Glancing at Clint with alarm, she saw trepidation and deep dread smoldering in his eyes. Slowly, she lowered her eyes to the page clutched in her shaky hand and read aloud:

"Tell him revenge is sweet, and falls on those we love."

CHAPTER FOUR

"Give me that!" Clint's face turned a deathly shade of gray as he snatched the page out of Elise's hand and stared with tormented eyes at the pasted letters. "Good God, it's even worse . . ."

Halting his thought midsentence, Clint reached for the envelope still clutched in Karen's hand. "No postmark," he gritted. He stormed to the window and peered through a crack in the curtain. "Someone hand delivered this."

"The man in the black car?" Elise wasn't certain where the shaky voice came from, but she awaited Clint's answer—any answer—with a dimension of fear that seemed set apart from reality.

"What car?" Karen demanded curiously, shoving her blond hair behind her ear.

Clint seemed lost in the world outside the curtain, and Elise swallowed back a wave of panic and stepped behind him. Touching his arm with apprehension, she made him turn toward her. "Clint, it said 'revenge.' What does that mean?"

Clint looked at her as if she were stolen goods he had to find a hiding place for.

"Clint!" Her voice was becoming raspier as the fear in his Cimmerian eyes more closely mirrored that in hers.

Roughly, he grabbed the phone, jabbed out a number, waited long enough for an answer, and punched out another group of digits.

"Clint, the mystery ends right now," Elise said in a tremulous voice, her eyes rimming in red as the sting of uncertainty filled them. "Tell me what they meant by 'revenge.'"

Clint slammed the phone down, letting the quick yet lingering ring of impact die away. "They meant that you're in danger, Elise," he bit out, his eyes turning violently darker. "They're after you too."

"But I didn't do anything!"

"You're someone I care about," he explained in a vicious whisper. "They'll use you to get to me."

"Who will?" she shouted from the brink of hysteria.

"I don't know!" he yelled back.

Incredulity sprang to Elise's eyes. "You don't *know?* Well, what *do* you know? How much trouble are you in, Clint? How badly do they want you?"

Karen clutched her forehead and stepped between them like a referee in a boxing match. "Wait a minute! This is beginning to sound dangerous!"

Clint swung toward her. "It *is* dangerous." He caught a ragged breath and gave a haunted look around the room, as if its very existence threatened them. "You can't stay here where they can get to you," he said in a more calculated voice. "You'll both have to come with me."

Elise felt as if the tension in her balled, shock-strained heart would cause it to collapse. "I'm not going anywhere with you!" she nearly screamed.

"Wait a minute!" Karen shouted again, stemming Elise's hysteria and forcing Clint to look at her directly. "What kind of danger are we talking about here? Getting eggs thrown at our cars, or our house blown up? Is this a matter of inconvenience or life and death?"

"Life and death," Clint said, unequivocally.

Elise shook her head, every fiber in her body denying the danger that was becoming apparent to her. But then she went to the telephone and grabbed the receiver. "I'm calling the police."

"There's no time," Clint said, taking the phone from her hand. The power in his action belied the gentleness in his voice. Quietly, he set the phone back in its cradle.

Elise looked at him with eyes that saw a different man than she had seen ten minutes earlier. "Clint, I am calling the police," she insisted. She reached for the phone again, but he grabbed her wrist and stopped her.

"Go get your things, Elise," he said. His breath was getting heavier, and she felt the slight tremor in his grip.

"No," she bit out. "Not until I've talked to . . ."

60

"For God's sake, Elise!" Clint grated in a booming voice. "Do what I say! Now! We have to get out of here!"

Elise jerked her arm away and stepped back, her eyes making a valiant attempt to assess this new version of Clint. "And what if I refuse to go?"

"I won't let you refuse," he warned. His face was reddening, and his lips were pressed tight against his teeth. "You have no choice."

Elise jutted her chin defiantly, and crossed her arms with a bravado she didn't feel. "How do I know that you aren't more dangerous than the person who sent that letter? How do I know it isn't some insane last-ditch ploy to get me back?"

"You *don't* know," he whispered harshly. "But I don't have time to convince you. You're coming with me if I have to knock you out and drag you."

Elise's back was ramrod straight, and her chin angled up another rebellious degree. "You wouldn't touch me."

"Elise . . ." Before Karen could voice the plea for silence that shone in her eyes, a roaring backlash of fire whipped across Clint's eyes, and he grabbed Elise. "You want to try me?" he asked in a strange, explosively quiet voice against her ear. "I've learned a few tricks while I've been gone, and developed a definite streak of impatience. If you really want to see how much a man can change after eight months of horror, then you just keep up this little fight and I'll show you."

"You're hurting me," Elise whispered.

"I'm trying to *save* you," he bit out, loosening his grip a degree without easing the controlling hold he had on her. "Karen, get her things and yours. We might be gone for a while."

Karen hesitated. "Like . . . how long?"

Elise felt his throat convulse against her head, heard his breath fulminate in a rush. "Look. I don't give a damn whether you even take a toothbrush! You have exactly sixty seconds to grab what you need or we're going without it."

Elise closed her eyes and struggled not to fall apart as Karen disappeared into the back of the house. Clint wrapped an arm across her chest and held her more like a lover cherishing his woman than a kidnapper clinging to his hostage. "Elise, you have to trust me," he whispered against her ear. "You have to . . ."

"Let go of me," she whispered. "I don't want you touching me. You're despicable, and dangerous, and—"

"Elise, it isn't me. You don't understand." His pleading voice against her ear almost made her want to understand, almost made her trust him, almost made her unafraid.

Until the telephone rang, recreating her hope and shattering it at the same time.

"You can't answer it," Clint said, his arm tightening on her. "You aren't supposed to be home. They could be checking—"

"It's probably my studio," Karen said, rushing back in with two packed duffel bags as the phone continued to ring. "I told them to call me if—"

Clint hooked her arm as she reached for the

phone, his eyes on the edge of violence. "I said to let it ring," he whispered slowly. "It's time to go." He swallowed and steadied his voice.

"We're going to go out the same way Elise and I came in." He set an arm on each woman's shoulder in a brotherly gesture that could turn forceful instantly. "Open the door, Elise. And move fast."

Elise obeyed the order and pulled the door open. When they were outside, the three of them running through the backyard like soldiers expecting sniper fire, Elise felt as if someone else occupied her body while she stood outside it, watching the man she had once loved turn into a quiet lunatic who treated her like an unexpected hostage. For that was exactly what she was.

Elise tried to make eye contact with the strangers they passed when they reached the Bronco in the parking lot, but each seemed too caught up in his own life's worries to notice the cry for help in her eyes—a cry for help she was afraid to put voice to for fear that a worse danger awaited her if Clint was right. Clint opened the driver's door and shoved them in. "Get down on the floor," he ordered. He slid on his sunglasses and his hard hat. "And stay there no matter what happens."

"What . . . what are you expecting to happen?" Karen asked in a carefully composed voice.

Clint didn't answer. Elise hunched against the seat and stared up at the stern, gruff set of Clint's jaw, the glacial blackness of his eyes, the stiff set of his mouth, as he cranked the engine and set the car into motion. His eyes shifted back and forth

63

from the rearview mirror to the side streets as he drove, as if he expected an attack at any moment. Hard, tense muscles bulged through his clothes, testimony to the newer, more defined strength she had felt when he'd held her. He was a different man, she thought with a shudder. The old Clint had been sensitive, gentle, selfless. There had been no hint that beneath it all was violence and terror that could make him capable of . . . Elise's heart sank as she imagined the things he could be capable of now.

But when he glanced down at her, hunched next to Karen on the floorboard, that sharpness in his eyes vanished, and he swallowed. For a moment a deep surge of sadness sliced through her. That glimmer of regret in his eyes cost her her strength and her hatred, and she felt only a deep, yawning void with no hope of being filled, and the fathomless need to see the Clint she loved in that hard, unyielding countenance again.

Clint didn't look at her again, for the fear and sorrowful astonishment in her eyes tugged at his heart and distracted him from his purpose. He watched the trees as he whizzed past them, as if they were the enemy waiting for him. But somehow, in light of the things he had said and done to get the two women out of the house, he felt as if *he* were the enemy—theirs as well as his own.

Karen's look of composure and patience disquieted him, for he knew her mind too well. Elise was probably struggling to understand the image of a new, violent Clint, but Karen was more objective. She was turning the few facts she knew

64

over in her mind, he thought, trying to concoct an escape plan for the first opportunity that arose, gauging Clint's love of Elise against the bleak determination in his eyes.

Maybe, he decided with a dismal ache in his soul, it was time to reveal his pistol. Maybe then they'd both believe him capable of carrying out his threats, despite his deepest feelings.

He mouthed a curse at the idea that it had come to this. Elise was already afraid. The sight of a Magnum .357 would terrify her. When she'd known him—really known him—he hadn't even hunted. And now he stalked and hid like a mercenary, and she would see herself as his booty. That almost made him want to turn the gun on himself. And he would do that before he'd threaten her with it. Still, the sight of the gun might be threat enough to keep her and Karen from trying some fool escape that would get them all killed. What did he have to lose, after all? Her trust? His heart sank lower when he silently admitted that he'd lost that eight months ago.

Elise's haunted eyes followed the hand gliding the length of his leg, down the tight denim and over his knee, further to the ankle. Clint swallowed as he gathered up the calf of his jeans, revealing the leather holster strapped to his leg, and closed his hand over the small black gun. Elise's heavy release of breath, as if she'd expected as much from him, almost made him leave it where it was. But it was for Karen that he pulled it out and held it in his lap, aimed at his door. A deathly quiet, broken only by the sound of the engine, fell over them for a moment, but he kept his dull, lackluster eyes on the road.

Karen wilted and dropped her head into her knees, as if a million plans had just been shelved, but Elise's eyes grew colder and more determined *not* to wilt. "What have you turned into?" she asked beneath the volatile roar of the engine.

Clint didn't allow himself to meet her eyes. "A survivor," he answered with metallic certainty. "And I've had lots of practice."

Clint tried to harden himself to the harsh pair of blue eyes boring into him with hatred as emphatic as the love he'd known harbored there. It seemed that time stood still as she made her chilling assessment of him, the fear in her eyes not as great as the despair. But until he had them all within the bounds of safety, he could do nothing to change those opinions.

"Where are you taking us?" Karen asked wearily, as if she had nothing left to lose.

"We're meeting a friend who can get us safely out of town," he said. "I called him from your house and punched out a code on his beeper. He'll be waiting."

"Wonderful," Karen mumbled. "Another one just like you?"

Clint shrugged. "I ought to warn you, Karen. Sam'll see the two of you as just another problem to deal with. If I were you, I'd keep my mouth shut when I met him."

Elise's delicate nostrils flared a degree, and she seemed to sit up straighter in the small space allotted her. "If we're such a problem, then why didn't you just leave us?"

Clint turned off of the road and started a bumpy journey beneath a thick ceiling of pines that Elise could see from the floorboard. "I've told you why," he said.

The Bronco stopped, stemming Elise's comment, and Clint said, "You can get up now."

The scent of honeysuckle and magnolia blossoms filled the air, and the soft, comforting sound of rustling summer leaves and flitting birds played on her senses, calming her heart. Elise inched up and saw that they had parked in a small clearing surrounded by walls of sweet gums and blossoming dogwood and a forest of towering pine trees. A navy blue van waited opposite them, and the brown-haired man Elise had seen glimpses of for the past day and a half leaned idly beside it.

"Aw, hell, Jessup," Sam blurted when he saw the two passengers. "Does this look like some kind of party to you? Nobody told you to bring guests."

Clint got out of the Bronco and leaned back wearily against it. "I had no choice."

"Like you had no choice but to leave the treatment station when I told you to stay put?" Sam flared. "Like you had no choice but to play sitting duck without any safeguards at all while I was losing that guy? You pull that again, pal, and I may not show up to bail you out."

Clint sucked in a fathomless breath and thrust the threatening letter toward Sam.

"Terrific," the man muttered without surprise as he read the note. Gray eyes focused disgustedly on a tree-mottled sky. "Not only do we have to pull a vanishing act in broad daylight, trying to keep our lives intact, but we also have to worry about keeping them in one piece too. And they don't exactly look like willing participants. I told you it was a mistake to come back when you did. But what do I know, right?"

As if the man's ramblings were nothing new and therefore not worth acknowledging, Clint opened the van doors and looked inside, then dropped his head in a fatigued slump. "You could have at least gotten something with seats," he said. "It might be a long ride."

Sam made an up-and-down assessment of Elise, then Karen, his cool, sterling eyes telling them they were a burden that he did not welcome. "Who knew we'd have company? They can sit on the floor," he said.

Elise opened her mouth to lash out, but Karen beat her to it. "Look, mister whoever-you-are. This is no picnic for us, either. If you don't want any crashers in this little game of yours then just leave us and we'll walk home."

Sam uttered a low, dry laugh. "Lady, it sounds awfully tempting. But I'm not in the business of throwing pretty little appetizers to the wolves. It's my experience that it only makes them hungrier for what they're really after."

Clint clutched the roof of the van with both hands and glanced over his shoulder. "Come on. Get in."

68

Elise planted her feet and refused to move, and Karen followed her lead.

Sam stepped toward them, silver eyes conveying his volatile lack of patience. "The man said to get in."

Still, Elise didn't budge, and she mentally dared anyone to try and make her step into that van. Sam started toward her to meet that silent challenge, but Clint stopped him. "I'll handle her." He looked at her for a moment, but swallowed back the emotion that he had no time for, and scooped her up.

"Get your hands off me!" she railed, struggling to beat her way free of him. And Clint acquiesced, depositing her with a thud onto the bare metal floor of the van.

With a slight grin, Sam stepped toward Karen, but her gritting, "Don't you dare touch me," warned him off, and she climbed into the vehicle of her own volition.

"You won't get away with this!" Elise sputtered as they slammed them in and climbed into the front. "My father will have the entire police force looking for us before it even gets dark." The words were empty, she thought, for she often went days without talking to him, and he wasn't likely to realize she was gone at least until tomorrow. But the two men abducting them didn't know that.

"Yeah, yeah," Sam said, as if he'd heard it all before. Then he cranked up the van and started toward the highway.

Through eyes misty with fury and betrayal,

Elise watched Clint settle onto the floor where the passenger seat should have been and lean back against the door of the van, covering his face with a hand. The new life-style didn't come easily to him, she thought. There was at least some degree of suffering that went with it. She watched his chest heave, as if the weight of breath was too heavy. He leaned forward, hiked up the jeans on his right leg, and returned the gun to its holster.

Closing her eyes, Elise fought the tears that would reveal her shock, her fear, and her rage. It was best to retain a neutral expression at times like these, she told herself, even if everyone knew she was faking. She had learned that from her father long ago.

Her father, she thought. What would he do with that generous, misplaced forgiveness he'd had toward Clint just hours ago? But then, who would have ever believed that Clint had changed so drastically?

Forcing her eyes to the world whizzing by outside the van, she wondered in anguish where the road had turned. What had happened to transform the man she would have spent the rest of her life with—the generous, kind, sharing man she had been head over heels in love with?

A fleeting memory came back to her of the Christmas before last, when he had dressed as Santa Claus and taken gifts at his own expense to the patients in the children's ward of the hospital. He'd told her that night of the younger brother he'd had who had died after a long hospitalized illness, and the way he had never been able to forget the loneliness and boredom that had laced those last few months for the little boy. He'd never gotten over the need to find that younger brother in someone and offer the comfort and sunshine his own brother hadn't been able to accept. So he tried to brighten the lives of the children confined during the holidays. She wondered now if he had remembered that ritual last Christmas, or if he'd been too caught up in his new troubles to think of anyone but himself. Was that man still there beneath the harsh, cold shell of the criminal with the gun strapped to his leg and the eight months of mystery in his eyes? Or was this all that remained?

Karen nudged her out of her miserable reverie, and gestured toward Clint with a nod of her head. "What did he do? Why are we running?" she asked in the quietest whisper.

Elise gave a helpless shrug. "I wish I knew," she said on a sigh.

"If we just knew what we were up against . . ." Karen's words trailed off as Clint opened his eyes. He stared at Elise for a moment, his eyes two eloquent black gems. Then he moved toward them, and sat before Elise with his hands clasped between his bent knees.

"Elise, I know you're afraid," he said in a soft voice that was barely audible over the road noise. "I'm afraid too. But I want you to trust me."

"Famous last words," Elise muttered. "Kidnapping me or my roommate is not the best way to win my trust, Clint."

71

Clint mouthed a curse through his teeth. "Elise, whether you can believe it or not, I'm doing this because I love you."

Something in his eyes when he uttered the words tugged at Elise's heart, silencing her comeback, but Karen was unaffected. "Give me a break," she moaned.

"Just tell me what you did, Clint." Elise's plea came on a long sigh. "Make me understand what's going on here."

Clint kneaded his eyes, leaving them red. "Not yet. There's no telling what could happen before we get out of town. It's best if you don't know."

Elise closed her eyes.

"Trust him," Karen said sarcastically.

"The bottom line," Clint said in a bolder voice, "is that you *have* to trust me. Both of you. You simply don't have a choice. At this point there is nothing else you can do for yourselves." Then, as if there was no point in continuing the conversation, he turned away and went back to the door.

"There's something we can do for ourselves, all right," Elise whispered to Karen when he was out of earshot. "And we're going to do it as soon as this van stops."

CHAPTER FIVE

The ordeal seemed to shift from frightening to downright intolerable when Sam began to sing "Betty Lou's Gettin' Out Tonight," butchering the Bob Seger tune as he puffed on a cigarette between bars.

"Please!" Karen grunted over the van engine's straining back-ups. "This is enough of a nightmare without your singing."

Sam glanced over his shoulder, an amused half-grin working at his profile as he chanted the lyrics again, louder and even more off-key than before.

Elise buried her face in her knees and wrapped her arms over her head, but still the wailing continued.

"Give up, Karen," Clint moaned from his position on the floor. "I've been listening to it for months. He sings when he's nervous . . . or bored . . . or tired . . . or happy . . ."

Sam arched an undaunted brow and did a drumroll on his steering wheel, humming loudly.

"He would have been a rock singer," Clint explained, "except that he lacked one crucial element called talent, plus he can never remember the lyrics."

"Just for that," Sam said in a mock wounded tone, "I'm going to have to do my new and improved version of 'Just a Gigolo.' "

"First they kidnap us, then they torture us," Karen mumbled.

Sam cocked a brow and exhaled a stream of smoke. "Torture does sound intriguing. I'll have to consider it after we change to the camper."

"What camper?" Clint perked up at the new development.

"The one that should be waiting for us not too far from here. The one with all the comforts of home."

"Whose home?"

"Mine," Sam said.

"No offense, but you don't have a home."

"I don't know how to break this to you, buddy, but neither do you."

Clint gave a gentle shrug at the bantering, but both men seemed to sober for a moment.

Elise nudged Karen. "This is the time," she whispered. "Pretend that we won't give them any trouble, then when they let us out we can tell them we have to go to the bathroom and make a run for it."

"Be serious," Karen returned. "Don't you think these guys can outrun us?"

"Maybe they can," Elise said. "But if we have a few minutes' head start we might get to safety before they can find us."

74

The road turned rocky, and the interior of the van darkened as they entered another wooded area and wound down a path that didn't seem at all suited for such a vehicle. Branches scraped against the sides of the van, and the sound of gravel under the wheels sent a shiver up her spine. How far into these woods would they take them? she wondered frantically. And how in God's name would they ever get back out if they did escape?

Calm down, Elise, she told herself. There must be some semblance of a path, otherwise the van wouldn't be able to get through at all. They could just hide until Clint and Sam gave up on them, and then follow the path. *Don't be ridiculous,* she reminded herself. Clint wasn't going to give up. Not unless his danger was so immediate that he couldn't risk wasted time.

The van came to a halt, and Sam and Clint hopped out and slid open the side door. "Let's go," Clint said, holding out a hand for Elise.

Elise stepped down. The forest surrounding them this time seemed rougher and more primitive, as if it was rarely visited by the human species. But there had to be a way out, she told herself, for they weren't far from the highway. "I . . . I need to go to the bathroom," she ventured.

Clint gave a sarcastic laugh. "If you see one around here, you're welcome to it."

Elise gave the area another assessing look, and fought back the fear of what lurked there. If she were left there and couldn't find her way out

75

. . . That was silly, she told herself. She wouldn't be left here. She could figure out the way to the highway if she tried. It couldn't be more than a mile . . . "I really have to go," she said.

"So do I," Karen echoed. Her face reddened with the lie, and Elise feared it would give them away.

Clint cast Sam a suspicious glance, but Sam didn't seem to see a problem. "Fine. I'll go with you."

"You will not!" Elise barked.

Clint took Elise's arm. "I'll take her and you take Karen."

Elise shook her arm free, training her breath to function normally. "Look around you, Clint. Do you really see any possibility of escape? There are probably snakes in there, not to mention other rabid, hungry animals. Would I really be foolish enough to risk getting stuck here overnight?"

The plea was convincing, so much so that Karen's face faded to a translucent white.

"Just let the two of us go together," she pleaded. With a trembling hand, she touched Clint's chest, attempting her best shot. "Clint, it's been a horrible day. Please. It's not a lot to ask."

Clint heaved an impertinent sigh, his emotion at obvious odds with his intellect. "All right," he said finally. "Let 'em go. She's not stupid."

But Karen didn't look so sure. Sam released her, and she hesitated when Elise began to tromp off in the direction that seemed least dangerous— an area of the woods with thorny arms of bushes

76

and matted vines webbed between the trees. When Elise gave Karen a prodding look over her shoulder, she reluctantly began to follow.

"All right," Elise whispered when she'd caught up to her and they were pushing limbs aside as fast as their arms would move. "As soon as we get far enough away that they can't hear, we're going to run."

"Where?" Karen asked in a high-pitched whisper. "I don't know where we are. Do you?"

"We'll figure it out," Elise assured with pretentious equanimity.

"But it'll be dark in a couple of hours. What if we get caught in here overnight? What about those rabid, hungry animals you mentioned a minute ago? I'm not so sure I wouldn't rather be with Clint and Sam."

"How can you say that?" Elise hissed. "They have guns. They're taking us to God-only-knows where. They're making us accessories to whatever they've done."

"We're not accessories. We're victims," Karen argued. "And a guy who sings 'Betty Lou's Gettin' Out Tonight' couldn't be that dangerous."

Elise had never wanted to strangle her best friend more. "Karen, even if we could be sure they wouldn't hurt us, they are obviously not the only ones involved. There are others. Someone left that camper for us. How do you know they aren't dangerous?" Elise led Karen at a brisk pace while they whispered, brush crackling underfoot as they hurried over it. An unseen evil scraped Elise's arm, drawing blood, but she tried

77

to ignore it. Her eyes darted from left to right, straining for some idea of an escape route. As if by miracle, she spotted a dry spring that cut a path of earth through the trees. She turned around and held a branch up for Karen to duck under.

"Look, there's a clearing between those trees. Looks like a spring might have been here once. We could jump down in it and run as fast as we can that way until we reach the edge of the woods. Then we're safe."

Karen eyed the beveled, leaf-filled ditch and brought troubled eyes back to Elise.

"Karen, are you with me or not? We have to go now."

"Okay," the woman finally agreed, though every nuance of her expression indicated fierce doubt. "Take off. I'm right behind you."

Elise skidded down the incline to the dry spring and started to run as fast as her legs would carry her. Two years of jogging might have put her in shape for this sort of thing, she thought as she leapt over rocks and roots. But her sparse diet for the past two days, her sleepless night, and the strain that had been tearing at her muscles all day put her at a grave disadvantage.

Somewhere in the distance behind them, she heard her name being called in anger, and forced her legs to move faster. She heard Karen stumble and fall, whisper an appropriate expletive, then begin to run again.

The sound of distant car engines caught her attention, telling her that the highway was not far away. She strained her ears and listened for the direction, but Clint's voice came threateningly behind her.

"Damn it, Elise! You're going to get yourself killed!"

"This way," she whispered to Karen. "I can hear the highway."

They scurried up the side of the ditch and tore out through the thick walls of trees, vaulting in the direction of the road sounds that seemed even closer. But progress was slower, for nature prohibited them from getting through without stopping every few minutes to make passage.

"Over there!" she heard Clint yell to Sam, too close behind them.

Elise hurled her body through the brush, ignoring the way thorns clung to her clothes and snagged her skin. She came upon a drop-off, and told Karen to jump.

"But it's an eight-foot fall, at least," Karen whispered.

Elise ignored her and jumped, landing in a springing position that tested every muscle in her body. Karen followed, but her landing was not as graceful. She fell, sprawled, her knee twisted beneath her. "Oh, damn it!" she shouted.

"Can you walk?" Elise asked frantically. "Can you get up?"

Karen pulled herself up and tried to take a step, but her knee gave way.

The sound of cracking branches, running feet, and mumbled expletives reminded them of their urgency. "Go ahead, Elise," Karen whispered. "You're almost to the highway. I'll be all right."

Elise wrapped her arm around Karen's waist and tried to help her. "No. I'm not going without you."

"For heaven's sake," Karen pressed. "It won't do any good for us both to get caught. At least you can go somewhere and call the police."

The sound of the two running men grew closer, and Elise hesitated.

"Elise, use your head. Get out of here!"

She looked above her and saw Sam come into view. "There they are!" he shouted.

"Run, Elise!" Karen ordered.

Torn, Elise saw Clint running toward the drop-off as if to jump, and she turned and bolted into the woods, running as fast as she could go. The highway sounded within feet of her. Perhaps she'd make it. But behind her she heard Karen yelling and sobbing, and Clint's heavy footsteps gaining on her.

Twenty yards ahead she saw the trees thinning, heard the sound of an eighteen-wheeler rolling by, and felt the first bit of relief she'd known in hours. But suddenly Clint was behind her, his footsteps pounding the earth like foreboding thunder that stopped only when he caught her and dragged her down beneath him.

A scream tore from her throat, but he slapped his hand over her mouth and tackled her to the ground, the heavy weight of his body anchoring her against her will. She struggled with all her might and squirmed out from under him, scrambled to her feet, and started to run again. But Clint caught her leg and wrestled her down once more. Grabbing both of her arms, he threw her onto her back and straddled her, his weight keeping her from breaking free. "Don't . . . even . . . think about moving," Clint ordered, his voice as cruel as she had ever heard it.

Tears of helplessness burst into her eyes and spilled over her cheeks. She turned her head away and shut her eyes.

"I love you, Elise," he whispered heavily. "Don't make me hurt you."

Copious tears ran down her cheeks, and a sob burst from her throat. "There is no way on this earth you could hurt me more than you already have," she said.

She opened her eyes and stared at Clint, watching a look of sympathy flash across his face, a look brought on by her tears and vulnerability. He let go of one of her arms and wiped beneath her eye with a knuckle. She moved her face aside. "I'm going to keep trying to get away from you until I do."

"And I'll have to keep stopping you," he said.

"You might have to kill me to do it."

As if the words recharged his anger, he got off of her and hauled her roughly to her feet. With his hand over her mouth, he pressed her head back against his collarbone, and clamped his other arm around her waist. In spite of her resistance, he pushed her in front of him.

Sam was waiting with Karen when they reached the drop-off that had been their downfall.

"Oh, Elise," Karen moaned when she saw that she'd been caught. "You were so close."

Sam and Clint exchanged sober looks. "Get up, Karen," Clint said. "We're going back to the camper."

Sam shook his head with something nearing disgust in his eyes. "She twisted her knee. A little souvenir to remind her of her stupidity. I'll have to carry her."

"We'll follow this drop-off until it's low enough to climb," Clint said, his bass voice deep and intimidating against Elise's ear. His hold tightened on her waist, and his hand remained over her mouth. "We're going to walk now," he told her. "I suggest you use your feet, because I don't intend to be real gentle about dragging you."

Elise obeyed, though her eyes, now dry and alert, kept a constant lookout for some other escape route. Another one would arise soon enough. When it did, she would be ready. And no matter what the cost she would risk it. For she had no intention of falling under the power and dominance of the dangerous criminal wearing the face of the man she had loved.

CHAPTER SIX

Clint forced out a rending, fathomless sigh and looked toward the camper where he had just locked Elise, knowing she would try to get away again. But he was all out of threats. Short of actually hurting her, he didn't know how he could protect her.

"Did you hear me, Jessup?" Sam asked.

"What?" He turned around to his friend, stooped in front of Karen.

Sam shook his head. "I said that nothing's broken. It's just a little sprain, but it should keep her from pulling another stupid stunt for a while."

"Yeah," Clint mumbled. "But what's to keep Elise from it?"

"That lock on the door, for one thing," Sam said.

Clint closed his eyes and rubbed them roughly. Damn, he hated having her detest him that way. He hated the look he'd seen in her eyes when he'd locked her in, the look that said, "I loathe you and I'm afraid of you and I'll do anything in my power to be away from you." He hated that she didn't trust him enough to believe him when he said they were in danger, not from each other, but from someone else. But how could she trust him? *There's no way on earth you could hurt me more than you already have.* Her words raged in his mind, until he wanted to throw in the towel and walk out into the line of fire and die. She was all that kept him from it, all that had for eight long, empty, agonizing months.

"I'm riding in back with her," Clint said in a distant voice the moment the idea occurred to him.

Sam stood up and surveyed the pensive lines etching at Clint's face. "All right. Then this one can ride up front with me. If we keep them separated, they can't put their pretty little heads together."

Color rushed back into Karen's cheeks. "I'm not riding with you. I want to stay with Elise. We're not going to try anything."

"Of course you're not," Sam said. "You got it all out of your systems, and now you're just as happy as a lark to go along with us, and you have some swamp land in Florida you want to sell me. You're riding up front. Besides, I think Clint can handle a few hours alone with Elise."

"Elise doesn't *want* a few hours alone with Clint," Karen snapped.

Clint lowered his focus to his battered shoes and swallowed, knowing she was right. "Just get in the truck, Karen. Let me worry about Elise."

Karen resisted when Sam tried to lead her toward the door. "Clint, don't you hurt her!"

"Get in the car, Karen," he ordered.

Tightening her lips, Karen obeyed.

Sam closed her in and gave Clint a long, probing look, then clasped his shoulder with a big hand. "Do me a favor and be careful, okay?"

Clint breathed a mirthless laugh. "Careful? She's defenseless."

"Oh, no, she's not," Sam said, his perceptive eyes locking with Clint's. "Around you, she's dangerous. She has the worst weapon of all. Don't let her use it."

Clint studied the sky and let a long, tangled sigh tear from his soul. "Sam, she's scared. She's my woman, not my enemy."

"Just the same," Sam said. "A lot's at stake here. Don't follow your heart. We've come too far."

And they had, Clint knew. They'd been together, he and Sam, throughout it all, and if anyone knew the price he had paid, Sam did. For he had paid too. "I can't stand her hating me like this. I never planned on all this when we . . ."

"I know, buddy," Sam said, "but you can't lose your purpose now. Don't tell her anything until we get where we're going. If, God forbid, something should happen along the way, their ignorance might be the only thing that keeps them alive."

Clint nodded blandly, hopelessly, and watched Sam get in the truck, humming the tune to "Let It Be."

* * *

Elise started when she heard the second car door slam, and wondered what they'd done with Karen. She pulled her legs up onto the bed and wrapped her trembling arms around her knees. How long would they be in this match box, she wondered. How far would it take them?

Glancing around, she took a quick inventory of the "luxuries" in the camper. A sink, a small refrigerator, a cabinet. Above her head was another fold-out bed, and across from her was a narrow closet. Getting up, she opened it and found it empty. She opened the cabinet below the sink and found several cans of food, a loaf of bread, some peanut butter. A light dawned in her mind, lending hope to her fragile heart, and she pulled open the drawer. Among the forks, spoons, butter knives, and can opener lay a paring knife. Quickly, Elise grabbed it and, following Clint's example, tucked it against her leg under her sock.

A shudder coursed through her at the thought of using it, and she sank onto the bed again. If it came down to it, would she be able to hurt Clint to get away from him? She leaned her head back against the wall and closed her eyes. She wanted to think she could, but for the life of her, she wasn't sure.

The door of the camper swung open, and she looked up to find Clint hunched in the doorway, his hair roughly tousled and his shirt hanging open.

"Wh . . . where's Karen?" she asked when he closed the door behind him.

"She's riding in front."

"Why?"

"Because I wanted to ride with you."

"That isn't necessary."

"Isn't it? Isn't it absolutely necessary to keep you from killing yourself trying to keep me from saving you?"

"Nobody asked for your protection, Superman. I'd rather take my chances."

Clint stepped further into the room and reached into the refrigerator for a beer. "You sound pretty sure of yourself for someone who's never taken a chance in her life until today."

Elise lifted her chin at the barb. "I took a chance when I got tangled up with you."

Clint popped the top, took a long swig of beer, and set it down. "I don't recall that you had any reservations at all."

Elise shrugged and looked out the window as the camper started to move. "Who knew what you were underneath? Who had any idea?" The words were said dejectedly, and they embraced Clint with cold tentacles.

"And maybe I was wrong about you all this time," he said, not believing a word of it. "Maybe that heart I kept remembering was nothing but ice and bitterness. Maybe all that 'for the rest of our lives' crap was just a line to get what you wanted at the time."

Some emotion seemed to show in her eyes, but instead of making them softer, it made them harder. "Maybe so," she agreed.

Clint gave an unconvinced grin and threw back

another swig of beer. "Maybe you knew all along that you were tangled up with some sort of gangster, and you needed the excitement in your life." He set down the beer can, considered it. "There were clues, you know. All those plans I used to be so engrossed in at work, they weren't really project plans. They were blueprints of banks. You probably thought I didn't have much money, but the truth is that I have millions stashed away in a Swiss bank account. Or did, until I busted that one too." He shrugged and looked back at Elise's cold, intransigent eyes. "Remember all those plants I kept in my apartment? They weren't really plants. They were just clever props where I hid the money. It worked out real well for a while, and I only had to kill a few dozen people. You probably thought I was at home sleeping when I wasn't with you. In reality, I was flying to distant parts of the globe to launder my money."

Elise bit the inside of her cheek in impatience with his outrageous story and looked out the window.

"Don't know why you never suspected anything," he said, shaking his head with exaggeration. "When criminal behavior is so deeply ingrained in someone, the way it is in me, it's really hard not to spot. Unless . . ." His eyes widened in feigned understanding, and Elise couldn't help looking at him again. "Unless you're a female thug yourself!"

She rolled her eyes and looked out the window again.

"Of course," Clint said, clutching his head.

"Why didn't I see it before? You and your father are in this together! That's how he made his fortune! He didn't inherit it, and being district attorney is just a front. In reality, he probably sells used cars to third world nations! I knew there was something fishy about that guy!"

"If you think your flip attitude is going to lighten up this miserable situation, Clint, you're wrong," Elise said, finally. "I don't find anything about this funny. I think you and your stupid tone-deaf friend are disgusting. As far as I'm concerned, I am a hostage, and you are a kidnapper. And when the police find us after my father realizes I'm gone, I'm going to help them put you away for the rest of your life."

Clint lost his zest for the part he'd been playing, and black currents of anger glittered in his eyes. "I'm not a criminal, Elise. I'm a victim. And I can't tell you how good it feels to know that the woman I planned to marry has such faith in me."

"Faith dies, Clint!" she returned. "And I take full responsibility for winding up where I have in this relationship. I should never have loved you, and I should never have believed in you. Faith is just a flimsy piece of self-betrayal, an excuse for not having to depend on yourself. I learned a valuable lesson when you disappeared, Clint. I learned not to believe in anything or anyone anymore!"

Clint's eyes were pools of anguish as he tilted his head helplessly. "I did that to you?" he asked in a raw, reticent voice.

"I did that to myself," she said numbly. And then she closed her eyes and banded her arms tighter around her knees, constructing steel barriers that no one was likely to break down.

"There's something I should warn you about," Karen told Sam as she watched the signs they whizzed past on I-20. They had just passed Hattiesburg, and were going south, but the knowledge did her no good at all. "I have a very low threshold for pain. Any minute now this throbbing in my knee is going to reach the unbearable point, and you'll hear some moaning like you've never heard before."

"A low threshold, huh?" Sam asked, raising a brow.

Karen looked at the ceiling, cursing herself for giving away her weakness. "Well, I could pretend to be brave. But under the circumstances, I don't see what good it would do me."

Sam winked at her. "Don't worry. If I decide to torture you, I'll go easy on the knee."

"That's reassuring," Karen said. Somehow, the torture threat didn't pack much weight when it was delivered with a grin that told her Sam would rather tickle her any day. She wondered if her hunch was well-founded, and decided to feel her way around him and try to determine just what kind of man he was.

"Torture women often, do you?" she asked as lightly as she could.

He gave her a mirthful glance. "Every chance I get."

His eyes were the color of a winter storm with the first sparkling rays of sunlight warming through, and they made her smile against her will. "Ever been photographed?"

"Torturing women?" His brown eyebrow cropped further upward with the question.

She rolled her eyes. "Or otherwise. I have a special interest. I'm a photographer, and I've never photographed a criminal before."

Sam laughed aloud. "And now that the opportunity seems to have dropped into your lap, you might as well take advantage of it, right?"

Karen shrugged and glanced out the window. The sign said POPLARVILLE, 42 MILES. "Something like that."

Sam considered the idea for a moment. "You could call it 'Kidnappers Have Feelings Too.'"

"Do they?" she asked.

He grinned. "Occasionally."

The beeper on his belt sounded, and Sam reached down and retrieved it.

"The little Mrs.?" Karen inquired.

"Yeah, sure," he said. "I told her never to call me when I'm working." He took the beeper and read the coded message coming across the tiny screen.

"Aw, damn," he mumbled. "We've got to turn around."

Karen sensed the sudden swing in his mood and thought it was best not to go on with the bantering. "Are we going home?"

He shook his head. "Just someplace different. I've got to find a phone."

* * *

Elise opened her eyes when she felt the camper stop, and a new wave of apprehension passed over her. "Are we there?" she asked Clint, who was sitting on the narrow counter looking out the window.

"No," he said. "I don't know why Sam stopped."

The back door opened, and Sam stuck his head in and gave Clint a quick, whispered explanation.

"He has to use the telephone," Clint said when he'd closed the door again. "He got a message on his beeper telling us to turn around."

She slid to the edge of the bed, her eyes suddenly more alert. "Are we going home?" she asked, just as Karen had.

"I don't know where we're going," he said. "We'll have to wait until Sam makes the call."

"You mean you take orders from someone else?" she asked.

"Does that surprise you?"

"It frightens me," she admitted. "What if he doesn't like the idea of your taking hostages?"

Clint gave her a wan smile. "I can guarantee you that he won't."

Elise swallowed hard and struggled with the fear drawing the blood from her face. "He doesn't even know us. What if he—?"

Clint twisted the chain on his neck and bent over to look out the window.

"He isn't going to let anything happen to you," he assured her. "He's as worried about your safety as I am."

92

"Well, that isn't exactly comforting, since you just chased me down in the woods," she snapped. "Is he as demonstrative in his 'worry' as you are?"

Clint turned back around to face her, his eyes slicing into her. "He has his own methods. I haven't always agreed with them at first, but he's been able to convince me so far."

Was it another threat? Elise wondered miserably. Was he telling her that if the order was given, he'd kill her? Or was he saying something entirely different? Closing her eyes again, she tried to deal with the hysteria threatening to conquer her.

The door opened again, and Sam leaned inside. "We have to go north. It might be a six-hour drive or more."

"What happened? Why the change?" Clint asked.

"A little matter of a bomb," Sam said in a metallic voice. "Nobody was hurt. We think it was meant as a warning. So we've come up with another place we haven't used before. Just tap on the window if you need something and I'll try to find a discreet place to stop."

The door closed again, and Elise's piercing, fearful eyes locked with Clint's. "A bomb? What kind of hell are you taking me to?"

Clint swallowed and sank down on the floor, leaning back against the door with his eyes closed. "My hell," he said. "For the past eight months."

CHAPTER SEVEN

Sam's face was grim and pensive when he got back in the cabin. "We're going to be driving for about six or seven more hours," he told Karen. "If your knee is giving you a lot of trouble, I'll try to find a place to get you some aspirin."

"I would be deeply indebted," she said, noting the subtle change in his mood.

"It might be a little while, though. This station is closed, so we'll have to wait for the next town."

"I'll survive," she said. She studied his rugged profile, the pensive way he rubbed his beard, the deep, laugh/frown lines around his mysterious eyes. His new mood scared her, and when she was scared, she talked. "So how is the Mrs.?"

"Dandy," he said. "She told me to pick up a loaf of bread and some milk."

"And did you tell her you were bringing guests home for dinner?"

"Yeah. I told her to get the dungeon ready and not to feed the alligators, that they were getting a special treat tonight."

Karen's fears lightened a degree, and she looked out the window. "Is there really a Mrs.?"

Sam grinned. "You mean are there really hungry alligators?" He glanced askance at her. "Do I look like the kind of guy who would throw a little blond beauty to the alligators without torturing her first?"

Karen smiled faintly. "Then you're not married?"

"Was once," he said, sobering. "It didn't work out."

Karen studied the sudden flash of vulnerability in his eyes, and suddenly she wasn't quite so afraid anymore. "Too many late hours and unexpected guests?"

"Something like that," he said seriously. "And the fact that she hated guns. Unfortunate, considering I practically sleep with mine." There was a note of regret in his voice, a flicker of bitterness, before he changed the subject. "Why haven't you been snapped up?"

"Haven't wanted to be, I guess," she said, finding her own sobriety. "I like being independent. No one to answer to, no one to depend on to be there and understand. If you get kidnapped or something, you don't have any explanations to make." She flashed him a quick look. "Not like Elise. Her dad will be pulling his hair out worrying about her. Calling the FBI, the CIA, the PLO, the KGB . . ."

"And you like knowing there's no one back home to worry about you?"

Karen nodded. "It just makes things easier to deal with, you know?"

"I know," Sam said, nodding. "I know."

It wasn't long before Sam pulled into a 7-Eleven parking lot and stopped the camper. It wasn't much, Elise thought, and she didn't know what town they were in, but it was a chance. The best one she'd had since this whole ordeal had started.

"I have to go to the bathroom," she told Clint, lifting her chin with wilting bravado.

"If you remember, I've heard that before."

"Well, it's true. It isn't like it's a new development in the human body."

Clint studied her for a moment, wondering if he could, indeed, trust her this time. He remembered her last desperate escape attempt, and realized nothing in her attitude had changed. "Elise, you don't have to keep trying to get away. You'll understand this all soon enough. You know I'm not going to hurt you."

"I don't know that," she mumbled. "I don't even know who you are anymore. And you've threatened to hurt me several times today. But that's not why I want to use the rest room."

Clint raked his hand through his hair and held her eyes in a searching embrace, then he gave a dull shrug and sighed.

"So are you going to let me go?"

The door to the camper opened, and Sam stuck his head in. "I'm getting Karen some aspirin for her knee and some gas. Anybody need any-thing?"

"We could use something to eat," Clint said.

Elise sat up rigid, realizing Clint was going to ignore her request. "Will you please tell him that I have to go to the bathroom?"

Sam laughed aloud and peered around Clint. "I've heard that before."

Elise's face stung red. "Are you people aliens or something? Don't you have bladders?"

Sam flashed Clint a surrendering grin. "She does have a point there, you know."

Clint nodded wearily and took her arm. "All right, Elise. But I'm going with you."

"Fine," she said, though she deflated inside. She'd worry about getting rid of him when she got there. Maybe there was a window, or some people . . .

Roughly, he held her arm and walked her across the dark parking lot. The store was flooded with bright lights that her eyes had to adjust to, and she tried to focus long enough to see if anyone was there who might help her. But she didn't have time. Before she had even made eye contact with the store clerk, Clint had hur-ried her into the corridor leading to the rest rooms. And there was no one there to think it odd that he followed her into the lady's room.

No windows, she thought, looking around the dirty room with a sinking heart. Jerking free of him, she went into the stall. She tried to close it, but Clint wouldn't let her. Amazed, she gaped up at him. "What do you think I'm going to do? Drown myself?"

Clint scanned the possibilities in the stall. When he was satisfied that there was nothing there that would help her, he stepped back and allowed her to slam the door. "All right, but you have exactly thirty seconds."

Thirty seconds! she thought frantically. She tore out the roll of tissue paper and searched for something, *anything,* that would give her an idea for escape. But there was nothing. *Nothing!*

Nothing except the knife tucked in her sock. With a trembling hand, she took it out and examined it. It shone with a gloss that twisted her soul. What would she do with it? Threaten him? He'd wrestle it away from her in a minute. No, if she used it, she would have to mean business. She would have to use it the moment she opened the door. She would have to hurt him.

"Fifteen seconds," Clint said.

Elise closed her eyes and struggled with her choices. It might be her only one. And yet . . . she couldn't do it. As frightened as she was, she couldn't hurt Clint. Hating herself violently, she slipped the knife back into her sock and racked her brain for some other way. The person in the store was her only answer. She'd pretend to shop for something to eat, and somehow she would let the clerk know she was being held against her will. It was risky, and it might not work, but it was better than using the knife.

Just as Clint ticked off, "Five seconds," Elise came out of the stall. Brushing roughly past him, she washed her hands slowly, trying not to tremble.

Then she pushed out of the bathroom and back into the store area. "I want something to eat," she said, trying to make eye contact with the clerk, who seemed deeply engrossed in a book she was reading.

"Sam got us something," Clint said.

"But he doesn't know what I like. I need something salty. Some pistachios. Do you have pistachios?"

The woman looked up and shook her head. Elise flashed her a desperate look, but the lady was undaunted. She merely looked back down at her book.

But Clint didn't miss it. "Come on, Elise. It was a good try," he said. He set an intimidating arm around her shoulders and started her toward the door.

Elise wasn't about to let it go that easily. "Lady, he's—"

Clint set his hand over her mouth, out of the lady's sight. "She gets feisty when she can't find any pistachios," he explained, though the woman didn't seem to care.

And with controlling force that had been worked into his muscular arms for months, he pushed her outside and into the camper. She landed on the bed with a bounce, and turned back to see his eyes burning into her with disgusted rage, but he didn't utter a word.

And for some reason that she couldn't name,

she felt unaccountably ashamed and deeply regretful.

Over an hour later, from where she sat, curled up in her corner of the camper, Elise watched Clint in his private torment, his head cradled on the heel of hands curled into fists. Her heart ached, and she didn't want it to. "That place where we were going. Is it where you've been staying all this time?"

Clint dropped his hands and his obsidian eyes meshed irrevocably with hers. "Yes."

"Did . . . did they think you were still there? Is that why the bomb?" The question came on a shaky husk of breath.

"I doubt it," he said. "They obviously knew I'd gone home or they wouldn't have sent that letter to you. Like Sam said, it was probably just a warning."

"A warning about what?" Fear sprang to her eyes, and she looked out into the night, stellar lights and natural shadows dancing by the window.

Clint didn't answer. He simply stared at her with eyes as opaque and soulful as the sky at midnight when the moon was held captive in a prison of clouds.

"Okay," she said with resignation. "You won't tell me. But can't you take their warning? Can't you do whatever it is they want so they'll leave us alone?"

"No," he said.

Her balled fist came down on the thin mattress.

"Damn you, Clint!" she blared. "How could you have changed so much? How could I have been so wrong?"

His eyes held hers for a long moment, two pairs of pain looking to each other for the only balm that could soothe them. But neither could give.

"You weren't wrong, Elise. I'm the same man I was the night of our engagement party, when we went horseback riding after everyone left, and I held you and loved you until the sun came up. I'm the same man who had to call you three times every night after I left you, because I couldn't stand being awake and not having you with me."

Elise swallowed the emotion blocking her throat and dropped her head to her knees. She heard Clint get off the floor, felt his weight move the mattress as he sat down next to her on the bed. A small light over the bed flicked on, lending just enough light for them to see each other clearly.

"Look at me, Elise. The same man." Elise reluctantly looked up again, and Clint's eyes were misty shards of midnight, cutting into her soul. Her own eyes filled, and she blinked back the evidence of her grief.

"Then what happened?" The question came in a raspy whisper, reluctant to know, yet desperate to.

"I can't tell you until we're out of danger. It's too risky."

Elise's eyes blurred as she looked at him. "Too

risky? Why? Are you afraid that if you tell me I'll see the real you even more clearly? Do you know that in all the time you were gone, it never once occurred to me that you had done anything criminal and could be hiding? The lowest thing I could come up with was that you'd been so overwhelmed with responsibility that you had to get away. But when you came back, it all came together, like whirling pieces of a horrible nightmare. Only I can't wake up. And it keeps getting worse!"

Clint lifted his hand to touch her hair, but stopped before it made contact. "It won't get worse, Elise. I'm here now."

"But I don't want you here! Don't you understand that *you* are the nightmare? You're dangerous, and secretive, and unpredictable! I don't know who you are, and yes, I'm scared to death of you."

Clint touched her hair, his rough, callused fingers pampered by its softness. "Baby, I'm not a criminal and you don't have to be afraid of me. You'll see that soon."

His touch sent currents of warmth seeping through her, and more than anything she wanted to bury herself in his chest and feel the security of his arms around her, telling her it would be all right. But she couldn't.

"Don't touch me, Clint," she whispered.

But his other arm came around her, forcing her to lean against him, coaxing her into laying her head against his bare chest and squeezing back the tears threatening to crush her. The power and insistence in his embrace terrorized her. Where would it stop?

"You say you don't love me anymore," he whispered. "But I know how hard it is for you to let go of things. You don't replace things in your life, Elise, and you never forget them. And when I kissed you this afternoon, before we found the letter, I was positive that you still love me. I'm still positive."

"You're wrong." Trembling like a child in the freezing rain, she tried to pull away.

Clint leaned toward her, his breath teasing her face with the slight scent of beer, and he swallowed. "I'm not wrong, Elise. I'm not wrong."

His lips seemed to outline hers without touching, and she closed her eyes, letting one renegade tear escape. "I love you," he whispered.

The moment of contact almost shattered her, for the kiss was so gentle, so sweet, that she found no trace of the violence she had sensed in him all day. But it was there, she told herself, lurking behind the tenderness, waiting to strike her when her guard was down. "Don't," she whispered through quivering lips. "Please, don't."

He let her go then, and pulled back, his brows knitted with pleading intensity. He slid his fingers down to the hand cupped around her shin, and measured the pulse beating erotically. "You can lie to yourself, Elise, but you can't lie to me. I've always been able to see right through those beautiful eyes. They've always given you away. Right now they're giving you to me."

"You're seeing your own illusions," she whispered. "I can't help that."

His hand trailed to the back of her calf as he leaned toward her and pushed her hair back from her face. "Do you know that I almost went mad with wanting you while I was gone?"

She closed her eyes and struggled with the incipient tears, and his hand slid under her pants leg to touch the bare skin of her calf.

"I kept thinking of how your skin felt, how it smelled, how it tasted. I kept thinking of your warm mouth, and how it was the only thing that had ever been able to warm the chill in me."

His voice was seductive against her ear, and she struggled not to let it move her. His hand moved up and down her calf. "The thought of holding you again was the only thing that kept me going. Without it, I would have—"

His grip tightened around her ankle, and with eyes hardening to circles of dull coal, Clint pulled down her sock and found the knife.

He held it up, and she snatched at it, fearing his wrath more than she had before. But he held it out of her reach. "What were you going to do with it, Elise? Cut me? Kill me?"

"I was going to protect myself," she said, springing off the bed. "You had a weapon! I needed one too!"

His eyes scorched her, and Elise faced off with him, her mind groping for a way to arm herself in the attack being launched in his eyes.

Behind her back, she reached to the sink for the gun lying there, but Clint didn't miss the movement. In seconds he had grabbed her and thrown her onto the bed, his body pressing her into the thin mattress, becoming more forceful and crushing the more she fought. He wrenched her legs apart with his to better control their thrashing beneath him, and held her arms away from her. Fury raged in her eyes, and her face washed crimson. "You can lock me up and threaten me and rape me and kill me," she hissed through her teeth, "but you won't get away with it. Somehow I'll get you back, Clint Jessup!"

"Rape you?" His voice came in an incredulous, breathless tone, and he uttered a low, disdainful chuckle. "Lady, I won't have to rape you. You won't fight me that long."

"I'll fight you until I die," she grated.

As if to prove his point, his mouth came down on hers, hard and unyielding, forcing her to allow him bold entrance. His tongue thrust against hers, and she tasted danger and ire, and power too strong for her to fight.

But she fought anyway. She fought the warmth raging up inside her from the vulnerable point at which he was cradled against her. She fought the numbness in her legs, and the pounding of her heart, and the need in her soul. And she fought *him* with every bit of strength she had.

His kiss delved deeper, stripping her senses, robbing her of every weapon she possessed. But still she beat at his ribs beneath his open shirt with all her might, tried to squirm out from under him, tried to make the task harder for him than it was for her. But his magic was too strong, and his threat had been too accurate.

105

Her body responded wildly, as her heart usurped her mind. His hands left her face as he felt the fight melting from her, and he trailed them down her sides and slid them beneath her. His wet lips trailed down her face, beneath her chin, to her neck, sending waves of shivers washing over her, dragging breath deeper and deeper from her lungs as he ground her against him.

She closed her eyes and tried not to whimper from the riot he incited within her, and she felt her hands sliding over his back, to the tight stretch of denim. As if her pleasure was the sole object of his force, he brought her rhythmically to dark, explosive heights, making her gasp for air, forcing her to abandon her doubts and cling helplessly to him.

When she opened her eyes again, his were misty, probing into hers with keen perception. "I'm not going to rape you, Elise," he whispered hoarsely. "I'm not going to do anything that you don't want me to do. But I want to make love to you. The choice is yours."

Self-disgust welled up in her chest, blocked her throat, drowned her lungs. Tears of self-recrimination rolled down her face. How could she have just reveled in the weight and motion of Clint's body, knowing what he was? How could she let her emotions and physical desire completely smother out her rationale? "I hate you," she whispered through grating teeth. "And I hate myself."

With a sad look that drove the life from her soul, Clint pulled slowly off of her.

CHAPTER EIGHT

The heat in the camper suddenly seemed stifling. Elise watched as Clint slung off his shirt and threw it in a wad to the floor, then braced himself over the small sink and turned on the water. She had wanted him. God, how she had wanted him, and if he had pushed just a little harder . . .

She laid her wrist over her eyes and gritted her teeth. What was she turning into? She had reacted to him as if nothing had changed. For a moment of pleasure, for a buried memory, she had cast aside her values and instincts and responded as she always had in the past. How could she still want him?

Looking out from beneath her hand, her eyes strayed to the bare, rippling muscles stretching across his back and shoulders, down the corded bulges of his arms, following the twisting lines of power down to his lean waist. The skin was bronze-hued and beckoned her touch, and she realized that if he'd been without his shirt a moment ago there might have been no turning back. In a mental caress, her eyes scanned the rear of those worn jeans, the faded places that stretched over the tight body they enhanced more than concealed. Was he still a gentle lover? Did he still remember all the ways he used to make her crazy?

She tightened her stomach and tried not to think how his body had felt just now over hers, how expertly he had rocked against her, how close he had brought her to abandonment. Strictly physical instincts, she told herself of her response. Nothing more. Nothing more.

Still, her eyes roved over him, gravitating back to the bare skin above his waistband, inching around his tight waist to the zipper . . .

She sat up slowly as a long, crooked scar just on the front side of his waist caught her eyes, and she inhaled sharply.

Clint heard the tiny gasp and looked toward her, saw what she had seen, and turned back to the sink. Self-consciously, he set his hand over the mark that started at his side and disappeared inside his jeans.

"It's a scar," Elise said, the statement a question in itself.

Clint nodded.

She slid to the edge of the bed, her eyes suddenly lacking the disdain he had seen there earlier. "Let me see."

Breathing a deep sigh of resignation, he dropped his hand.

Elise muttered a groan at the jagged cicatrix that hadn't been there before. "What . . . what happened?"

"It's a knife wound," he whispered wearily.

"Knife?" She choked on the word and blinked back the sudden ache of tears at the back of her eyes. "You . . . you were stabbed?"

"Do you really care?" he asked with all the misery his soul contained. "You would have done it yourself if I hadn't found your knife."

Elise gazed up at him, suddenly feeling the importance of making him believe she couldn't have used it. "No . . . I was just going to use it for self-defense if I had to."

His deep, unfathomable eyes misted, and he focused on the ceiling of the camper. "You know I'd rather die than hurt you."

Somewhere, deep within her, she did know that. She touched the scar with unsteady fingertips, and he sucked in a breath and looked down at her. "When were you stabbed?"

"Right before I left." His eyes said more. They told her that was why he'd disappeared, that there *had* been a valid reason.

"Who?"

He shook his head, denying her that answer. "Not now. Not yet."

A sob was rising in her heart, waiting at the back of her throat for her to give it voice. "You could have died," she rasped in a whisper.

"I didn't, though."

Despairing rivulets of tears painted her face, and she caught a fleeting breath and slid her arms around his hips. "You could have died," she said again.

She looked up at him, her chin pressed against

109

his stomach, and saw the pain tearing at his face, and suddenly nothing mattered anymore except taking it away.

Tentatively, she pressed her lips against the rugged line on his waist, and felt his abdomen tighten. He threaded his fingers through her hair and gave a moaning sigh—a sigh that said "thank you," a sigh that said "I need you," a sigh that said "love me." She shivered at the way her heart responded to that sigh. There was a reason, she thought with a heart-deep shudder. He had not abandoned her without reason. She was certain they were complex, mixed with fear and danger, death and pain—as complex as the love they had for each other.

Her lips followed the line down his side, and again she felt him suck in a breath. Her hands slid around his waistband and stopped at the button of his jeans. He caught his breath when she opened them.

"Elise, you're playing with fire," he admonished huskily.

Her fingers closed over the zipper, and she looked up at him, saw him close his eyes and swallow. The jeans parted, revealing the scar that tapered near his hipbone. Her lips followed its progress, bathing it in kisses, healing it with her tears. She felt the restraint, the arousal, the tremor, and she worked his jeans lower down his hips.

His moan at her ministrations gave her deep pleasure, but she found herself with fierce needs of her own. She pulled onto her knees, facing him, and began to unbutton her blouse, watching his smoldering eyes as they followed her progress impatiently. He reached out and slid the blouse off her shoulders, and pulled her against him. Their lips came together in quiet reunion, so gently that she forgot the fear and heartache and anger she'd felt that day, and knew only an insatiable yearning for the most precious man on earth—the man she would gladly have traded her life for over the past eight months, if she had only known he loved her.

His kiss trailed down her chin, and his callused hands slipped the blouse off of her. Deftly, he opened her bra, freeing her breasts, and his grateful sigh breezed across one budded tip before his mouth closed over it.

Fire burst through her in liquid rushes as his tongue controlled her. Shuddering, she brought his face back to hers, and his lips met hers in soft supplication, lowering her to the bed, anchoring her again with the gentle crush of his claim. His hair-roughened chest glided over her bare breasts as his kiss plunged deeper. Elise's hand caressed the scar that had given her a means by which to admit her love, and he moved his hand down to cover hers. "You're healing me, Elise," he whispered in a tone racked with emotion.

Fresh tears sprang to her eyes, and she met his, brighter than the brightest star nestled in the warm blackness of the sky. "I love you, Clint," she sobbed. "I never stopped loving you."

"I know," he whispered. "I know."

"I've wanted you since I saw you yesterday

. . ." she confessed, shaken and torn by the heights of feeling devastating her.

"I was yours," he said.

She slid her hand off of the scar and tried to rid him completely of the denim impeding her. "Make love to me now," she entreated with a tremor. "I need you."

His lips covered hers again with shattering pressure, leaving her aching for more. His hands molded and caressed the straining swell of her breasts. Then they trailed to her bare, flat stomach, to the waist of her jeans. With agonizingly slow movements, he opened the snap at her waist and peeled the zipper down. He lowered his face to her navel, circling it with devastating patience as a high, whispered moan uncurled from her lips. His hands slid the cloth down her hips, off her legs, and then his weight was on her again, sliding up her body, his lips lighting and suckling and feathering. She struggled to hurry him, but he was like a cloud flirting with the sea, drawing moisture from her depths to use for his storm.

When she thought her heart would not find the strength for another beat, he sat up and tore his own clothes off, eyes anticipating the union of cloud and sea. She followed the scar down his hipbone with a trembling hand, but she no longer found that pain in his eyes. Instead, she found passion-impatient, restless, frustrated desire. When he entered her, her own storm raged higher with his, whipping water into violent arcs that sucked the cloud lower, twisting and circling and dipping into a raging vortex that robbed them of thought and person. Together, they *became* the vortex, drawing each other into the bottomless whirlpool of passion, from which there would never be escape.

When the storm was spent, they lay exhausted in each other's arms until the trembling subsided and their breathing had settled. And Elise drifted into a sleep that erased all problems, while the looming cloud guarded the vulnerable sea.

"Don't you ever get tired of driving?"

Karen's question cut across the darkness and the road noise, and Sam glanced over at her. With a deep sigh, he said, "I get tired of a lot of things, but I still have to do them."

"But you've been driving for hours. And it's dark. And the Natchez Trace is so winding and eerie."

Sam smiled and patted her knee with bold familiarity that made her furious. "Thanks for worrying, honey, but I can handle it."

"I'm not worrying about you," she said in brittle rebuttal. "I'm worried about myself. If you fall asleep and drive off the road we'll all be killed. Why don't you let someone else drive for a while?"

A high-pitched laugh tumbled out of Sam's throat. "Someone like you?"

"No, I know you wouldn't trust me. But what about Clint? He could pull his own weight."

She could barely see him in the darkness, but she saw enough to know his face had sobered.

"Clint can't drive. It would make him an open target."

It took a moment for the words to penetrate, and suddenly Karen's eyes darted to the side mirror that gave a view of what was behind them. "Target for what?"

Sam didn't answer. His fingers curled more tightly over the steering wheel, and his eyes narrowed.

"Are you a target? Am I?"

Sam's finger began to tap, slowly at first, then more rhythmically. When he opened his mouth, Karen braced herself for an admission that she did not want to hear. But all that came out was a quiet, off-key, " 'Da doo ron ron ron, da doo ron ron.' "

Letting out an exaggerated sigh, Karen leaned her head against the window and closed her eyes. She blocked out the worry she had for Elise, trapped for hours in the back of the camper with Clint. She blocked out the dread of where they were going and what would happen to her there. It was easy to do, for she had done it all her life, ever since she was a child and her parents had died in a plane crash. She had learned to turn away from pain and worry when she went to live with a distant aunt who saw her as another duty God had thrust on her. Long ago, as a towheaded little girl, she had learned to concentrate on the present, and to take solace in whatever was at hand. Tonight all she had was a strange man who represented a mixture of danger and security, so she mentally turned to him, taking refuge in his

114

presence and the soft, repetitive sound of his voice.

Elise stirred in Clint's arms, and he looked down at her and kissed the top of her head. She slept so soundly when he held her. She always had. He studied the slumberous lines of her face in the dark confines of the camper, and thought how many times he had imagined holding her like this and just watching her until she woke.

A helpless feeling of loss overwhelmed him at the memory of the eight months that had separated them, when he had honestly believed that nothing ever would. But it was nothing so simple as time that had come between them, he thought, focusing on the ceiling. It was Jake Calloway.

Jake Calloway. The very name made his adrenaline shift into high gear, and he could feel his face warming with seething blood.

"Damn it." The words came unbeckoned from his lips in a harsh whisper, as they had done countless times in the last few months. How could such a chain reaction have started from one visit he paid to a stupid kid who'd left a vial of cocaine in the pocket of his lab coat at work? How could he have known that when he knocked on that door . . .

. . . there was no turning back. The knock on the door made it final, sealing the decision to confront Jake with his finding. Clint looked down at the vial in his hand and shook his head. It explained a lot of things. It explained Jake's sudden bursts of energy in the middle of the day. It explained his coming in late more and more often. It explained his distant preoccupation at times when he should have noticed important elements in their research. He would say it was none of Clint's business, and he would probably get angry. But Clint could live with that.

Because it *was* his business. He had grown fond of the twenty-year-old kid who reminded him of himself at that age. He didn't want to see him ruin his chance at a good career before it even got started. And Jake didn't have anyone else. No father or mother to straighten him out. In spite of the odds against him, Jake had done well. He was no genius, so he hadn't been able to rely on scholarships to get him through school. He had supported himself by working alternate semesters while he was working toward his degree. And he had done rather nicely, considering his low pay. Clint wasn't about to let him throw it away by getting drawn under the spell of cocaine abuse.

The door opened, and Jake caught his breath at the sight of Clint. "I . . . I thought you were someone else." Raking a distracted hand through his brown hair, the young man looked past him, his pale blue eyes darting up the street in front of his house.

"Can we talk?" Clint asked.

"No," Jake said quickly. "I'm expecting some people."

"Jake," Clint prodded. "It's important."

"Sorry, man. I'll call you later." The door

started to close in Clint's face, but he stopped it with his foot.

"I found something in your lab coat pocket, Jake," he said, undaunted. "And I'm not leaving until I talk to you about it."

"My pocket? Wh—?" The word got caught in his throat as Clint brandished the vial. With a rugged sigh that seemed more impatient than surprised, Jake stepped back and let Clint in. "I appreciate your returning it, but you can't stay."

Clint walked into the house that Jake had said he was taking care of while the owners were in Europe, and made a quick pan of the state of utter disregard for property—clothes strewn over chairs and sprawled across the floor, dirty dishes cluttering the table, glasses with cigarette butts floating in rancid liquid. Briefly, he wondered if the owners had expected this when they'd asked Jake to house sit. He turned back to Jake, who was at the window now, peering nervously out. "Man, I mean it. You have to *leave!*"

"Not until we talk," Clint insisted again. He sat down in a chair and leaned forward. "Jake, you don't need that stuff. You have a lot going for you, and I don't want to see you—"

"Okay, fine," Jake agreed, cutting him off. "I'll quit." He took the vial, rushed to the kitchen off the den, and poured it in the sink. Hurriedly, he ran some water down the drain, and came back to Clint. "See? It's gone. Now will you please go?"

"You expect me to believe that it's over just like that?"

Jake's face flushed crimson, and he banged his fist into a wall. "What do you want from me? A freakin' affidavit? I told you—" The sound of an approaching engine outside stopped his words, and he swung back to the window. "Damn it! I knew this would happen. Hurry up. Get upstairs! Now."

"What?"

"Hide upstairs, Clint! If these people see you, they'll kill us both. This is no joke. Get upstairs and hide in the bathroom. And don't come out under any circumstances."

"Jake, I'm not hiding anywhere—"

The rage in Jake's crimson face was urgent, desperate. "Listen to me! I'm trying to keep you from winding up just another unexplained stiff on the side of the road. Do what I say!"

The doorbell rang, and Clint began to believe the panic in Jake's eyes. "Please, Clint!"

Reluctantly, Clint started up the stairs, but he had not hidden in the bathroom. He had gotten out of sight behind the rail overlooking the lower level, and he had watched a scene played out that had played over and over in his head almost every day since. And it had cost him every ounce of peace he'd ever had in his life . . .

Peace. Lying in this moving camper in the night with the woman he loved in his arms was as close to peace as he could hope to be. But it was enough for now.

Elise's eyes fluttered open, the lashes tickling the hair on his chest. Her hand slid across his

118

stomach as she woke, arousing him all over again, as if he hadn't loved her only an hour ago. "Hi," she whispered.

"Hi." His voice rumbled deep against her hair, and his arms closed more tightly around her.

"I had a dream that we were married. That we were safe. That I wasn't so afraid of losing you." She looked up at him, her cerulean eyes washing through him.

"I'm not going anywhere," he whispered against her lips, but he wasn't sure he could carry out such a promise. And as he made love to her again, he realized how fragile life and love actually were. For they could be snatched away as quickly and effortlessly as a gunshot ringing in the night.

"'And she's cli-imb-ing the stai-her-way to heav-en . . .'"

The soft, gravelly voice cut into Karen's sleep, pulling her out of her restless nightmare of running through the woods and getting caught by the monsters who chased her. But it wasn't the voice that had awakened her, for she suspected there hadn't been much silence since she'd drifted off. It was the human warmth surrounding and supporting her . . .

She opened her eyes, and found herself curled up against Sam's chest. His arm rested comfortably behind her, and his big hand sat splayed on her hip.

"Well, if it isn't Sleeping Beauty," he rumbled.

Karen sat up and deliberately moved his arm off of her. "I . . . I didn't mean to . . ."

Sam chuckled under his breath. "Do I look like I have any complaints?"

"But . . . I don't usually . . ."

"Fall into the arms of strange men?"

Her face tightened with sleepy indignation, and Sam laughed again. "How's your knee?"

Thankful that he had the decency to change the subject, she glanced down at it. "Hurts a little, but it's better." She glanced out the window at the stygian blackness. "I hope Elise is all right."

Sam laughed. "Well, it's so quiet back there that they're bound to have either made up or killed each other."

"They haven't made up," Karen said on a yawn. "So they must be dead."

"Must be." Sam bit his grin as he glanced over at her, and Karen couldn't help laughing.

"You're crazy."

"So they tell me," he admitted.

A moment of quiet filled the cab, and Karen studied his unshaven profile, the hard, angular line of his nose, the sleepy flush of his cheeks, the ruffled disarray of his chocolate hair. But his eyes were awake, bright, comforting. "So," she said after a moment. "What are you going to sing for me now?"

A slow grin crept across Sam's face, and he gave her a wink. "Got any requests?" he asked.

* * *

Clint awoke to the sound of gravel cracking under their wheels, and he peered out the camper window to the small cabin lit up in wait for them. Several cars lined the gravel drive, and a small crowd formed on the front porch at their approach. The chill hand of apprehension clutched him at the sight of so many more men than had been with him before.

The camper stopped, and he heard Sam's door slam. Several of the men approached him, exchanged words, and then the back door opened.

"You awake back here?" Sam asked.

Clint rubbed his eyes. "Yeah. What's going on? Who are all these people?"

Clint saw Sam bite his lip distastefully. "He wanted us to beef up security since we brought our two guests with us."

"Security was tight before. It didn't need beefing up."

"Tell me about it," Sam said dryly. "But we could be guarded by every gun in America, and he still wouldn't think we were doing enough to protect his little girl. And he's running this show."

"Terrific," Clint said, looking down at Elise. She lay curled up under a blanket, her face warm and sleepily seductive.

"So how'd it go?" Sam's voice cut quietly across the darkness.

"Fine," Clint said. "She still thinks I'm some kind of criminal, but she's more afraid *for* me than *of* me now."

121

"She should be, pal," Sam said. "It's getting down to the wire now. We just have to hold out a few more days. Then it'll all be over."

The words left a hollow feeling in Clint's chest. Would it ever be over? Would he really ever be able to sleep at night without keeping one eye open for someone to spring at him out of the dark? He'd believed he was safe when he went home, but that hope had been shattered. Now his primary objective was to protect Elise.

"Give me a minute to get her awake," Clint asked his friend with a soft smile. "I'll be right there."

"Okay," Sam said. "But don't be too long. They have a lot of questions for us when we get inside. And I have a few for them."

Karen stirred when she felt the comfort of a bed beneath her, and a strong man's arms releasing her. The room was dark, but she looked up and saw the weary face of Sam, her captor, tucking her into bed. His silver eyes were shadowed, and the lines etched in his face seemed much more defined than they had earlier. He was bone tired, and yet he seemed to be concentrating all his efforts on covering her with the comforter he had pulled back. For a moment, she wondered if he'd crawl in next to her, or simply collapse beside her from sheer exhaustion. She felt the incredible urge to reach out and smooth his disheveled hair, but she pretended she was still asleep.

His heavy hand rested on her shoulder when the comforter was in place, and she felt his pause and his warm eyes studying her. What was he thinking she wondered with a burst of warmth? Was he attracted to her? Or was he wondering what he was going to do with her? Somehow, no matter what the circumstances were, Karen couldn't manage to work up any fear of him at all.

There was some emotion in its place, however, but she wasn't ready to name it yet. She'd do that tomorrow, she told herself as she drifted back to sleep.

In her dreams, an off-key humming set a rhythm in her heart, a soft lullaby that made her smile.

CHAPTER NINE

Clint looked down at Elise sleeping in the dark sanctuary of the camper, and wished he didn't have to wake her. She would be afraid of the people sent there to guard them. Even he couldn't put those fears to rest, for they became more defined when one knew exactly what the enemy was. The danger wasn't over by a long shot, and he dreaded going into the house with the new men that had been sent. How could he trust them to be on his side? With the exception of Sam, he had found it difficult to trust strangers ever since that night.

Sitting beside Elise at the head of the small bed, he leaned his head back against the wall and stared out the open door, wishing the scene wouldn't keep recurring in his mind. But just as it had unfolded in Jake's house, it came back to him now . . .

He had recognized Givanti, a state representative, and several big businessmen in the area. He remembered his utter disbelief when he'd seen the amount of cocaine about to be exchanged, then the onslaught of apprehension when an argument had broken out about the buyers not wanting to pay what Givanti wanted. And when Givanti demanded the full amount and named a meeting place for the exchange of the entire amount of cocaine the next night, the knowledge had grafted itself on Clint's memory.

He had watched as Jake's eyes darted nervously upstairs to make sure Clint was out of sight, and suddenly things became clear. So that was how Jake had paid for his sports car. And this house was probably his. And the clothes and trips.

The buyers had left, but the drama had not ended there. Clint continued to watch as one of the men turned on Givanti, accusing him of ruining the deal, and making threats about not bringing the cocaine he had in his possession to the meeting place the next night. The rest was a blur in Clint's mind . . . the scuffle between Givanti and the man he later learned was a schoolteacher named Anderson, the gunshot, the blood.

Fear had been an element that coursed through him like adrenaline when Clint realized that he would be next if Jake decided to expose him. But the young man had seemed too fragmented, and Clint suspected Jake was afraid for himself and the mistake that had made him a witness to the event. Whether it had been out of cowardice or the intention of dealing with Clint later, Jake had helped Givanti carry the lifeless body out without a word . . .

Clint took a deep breath and looked out into

125

the windy night. It had been just this peaceful that night, just this deceptively quiet when he'd slipped out of Jake's house and found his car on the opposite side from where Givanti and his men had parked. He had driven aimlessly, frantically, trying to decide whether to go to the police or to Elise's father, the district attorney. He had finally decided on the latter, hoping to tell his story to his friend and future father-in-law, instead of to a cold stranger in a uniform.

Elise had been asleep, but her father listened earnestly to the news and took a statement from Clint, then contacted the police himself. Mentally exhausted, Clint had slipped out of the house while Cranston was on the telephone, making plans for a major drug bust for the following night at the location Clint had given him. Looking back, he wasn't sure if it was simple fatigue or mental numbness in the wake of shock that had caused him to be so careless. But all he had wanted was to go home and sleep, and wake up to find it had all been a bad dream. And though it had occurred to him that Jake might be waiting for him, he had never suspected that the young man was capable of hurting Clint himself . . .

It smelled like rain, and the peaceful breeze sweeping through his hair had given him a false sense of security. He locked his car and slammed the door, and stood looking inside, seeing the scene yet again. A murder, he thought with a shudder. He had witnessed a murder. A man was dead, and he didn't even know his name.

He started toward his house, kicking at the pebbles lining the drive, and wondered if he'd handled it wrong. Perhaps it could have been stopped if he hadn't hidden, if he had let them know he was there. But then maybe he would have been killed instead. And maybe Jake too.

He flipped through his keys for the right one and stepped onto the dark porch. Feeling for the knob, he tried to insert the key, but a movement in the shadows caught his attention.

Jake was waiting for him, his dark, foreboding eyes angry and vengeful. And before Clint uttered a word, Jake rushed at him, and a piercing pain—jaggedly rending and as hot as scalding metal inside torn flesh—coursed through him, robbing him of response. He remembered stumbling and clutching at Jake's jacket, the questions caught in his throat, and the fear on Jake's pale face when he'd heard the wail of the approaching siren, the only thing that had saved him from another attack from Jake's knife. And he remembered Sam and another officer rushing to his aid, and pain fingering through him in a thousand different ways . . .

Somehow, Jake had gotten away. And Clint had little doubt that Jake would simply bide his time until he had another chance to kill him and, thus, save himself.

So Cranston had packed Clint into a trauma unit with Sam as his guard and a doctor at his side who kept him in a black fog until they reached temporary safety. It had been two days before his mind was clear again . . . clear enough to know that he was somewhere in south Mississippi with a battalion of stitches in his side, an IV running sustenance into his veins, and District Attorney Eric Cranston standing over him with the news that everyone involved, except Jake, had been arrested as the drugs were changing hands. Jake was still out there somewhere, a lurking threat to Clint's life. And for that reason, Cranston said, there could be no communication between Clint and Elise until after the trial. And that meant there would not be a wedding.

"I want her kept out of this," the older man told him with pain in his eyes, the only element that kept Clint from ripping out of his bed and strangling him. "Everyone has to think you got cold feet. My hope is that Jake won't tell anyone that you were the witness. If he didn't tell them in time to stop the exchange of drugs, he must have been afraid to confess that it's his fault there's a witness. If everyone thinks you just ran from the wedding, no one will connect you with this, and meanwhile maybe we can catch Jake . . ."

"But what about Elise?" Clint demanded. "What will she think?"

Cranston covered the uncertainty on his face with a trembling hand that betrayed his weariness. "We'll make her think the same thing," he said quietly.

"That I didn't love her enough to marry her? That I had to run?"

"It's better than letting her be used as a go-between. If she knows the truth, it will be obvious. She'll even try to come after you, or—"

The pain tore at Clint's side as he tried to sit up. "It won't work," he said, as if the simple words could make it true. "She'll never believe it. She knows how much I love her."

"Eventually she'll believe it," Cranston assured in a soul-sad voice. "And then when the trial is over . . ."

Clint dropped back onto the thin pillow beneath him, his eyes pleading with the district attorney's. "I was supposed to marry her this Saturday," he whispered on the deepest note of despair. "How can you take that away from us?"

"I love her," Cranston said. "It's that simple. And if you love her, you'll see my logic. A heartbreak is easier to heal than a knife wound or a million other dangers. She's my daughter, and I want her safe."

Eventually, he had seen Cranston's logic and agreed with it. Elise was safe, if nothing else. But he hadn't counted on it taking eight months for the case to get to court, or for the police's search for Jake to come up empty.

Empty, that is, until his body was found. Just last week, the police had found Jake's burned body after an explosion in an abandoned factory. Because Clint had threatened not to testify if they didn't let him resume his life, they had allowed him to return, under the misguided belief that Jake was the only one who had known Clint's part in the trial. But Jake must have told someone, he thought miserably. And his mistake of going back had cost Elise her safety.

He shook her gently, and she stirred. Lord, she had gotten more beautiful since he'd left, he thought. He'd never thought that possible, and he'd certainly never expected that his imagination had been so dull in conjuring up the true beauty she possessed.

The moment Elise realized the camper wasn't moving, she woke up. "Are . . . are we there?"

Where was "there" he wondered with a soft smile? What did she expect of their destination? A rundown deer camp in the middle of the north Mississippi woods, miles from any town? He doubted it. At best, she hoped they were home, he surmised. At worst, she probably expected a hotel. Not what had turned into an armed fortress against whoever wanted him dead. "We're there," he said softly. He touched her warm cheek and thought how long it had been since he'd watched her stretch to wakefulness. "But before we go inside, I want to warn you. There are men with holsters strapped to their chests in there. But you don't have to be afraid. They're not here to hold you hostage. They're here to protect us both. Your father sent them."

Elise bolted upright on the bed, her eyes two rounded sapphires. "My father?"

"Yes. He knows where we are. He arranged for us to hide here."

"My *father?*" The words came out on a shaky, disbelieving breath. "My father is involved in this?"

130

"Yes." He silenced her with a fingertip to her lips. "I'll tell you every—"

"How long?" The question was uttered too loudly, and she grabbed Clint's arm and shook him. Her eyes blazed with fear and betrayal, and he knew he couldn't keep the truth from her any longer. "How long has my father been involved?"

"Since the beginning."

Elise was struck with muteness, a suffocating clog at the back of her throat blocking out response.

"He wanted to protect you," Clint said in a voice meant to be soothing.

"Protect me? He wanted to protect me?" She shook away from Clint and stood up. "I'm sick to death of being protected! And lied to! And afraid! No wonder he was so worried about my reaction to your leaving. No wonder he wanted me to forgive you! Clint, why didn't you tell me this before?"

"I couldn't tell you everything when I didn't know if we'd make it here or not. I didn't want you just knowing that much, and thinking all the way that your father was some kind of criminal too. You'll understand in a minute." He touched her face, the gesture bestowing his promise to make things clear. "We'll go inside and get some coffee, and then I'll tell you everything."

Tears sprang to Elise's eyes. Suddenly, she wasn't sure she wanted to know. It had been hard enough to accept that Clint was involved in something of such proportions, but her father?

"Where's Karen?" she asked, as if the change in subject could erase the reality.

"Sam took her in. She's probably sleeping."

"She's probably scared to death," Elise said. She wrapped her arms around herself, trying to stop the sudden shivering. "I want to see her."

"All right."

Clint stood up and took her hand, but she jerked it away. She winced at the miserable action and closed her eyes. She had made love to him. She had told him she loved him. She had begun to trust him. And she still did. But somehow the new development, her father's involvement, confused her more than before.

"Elise, don't pull away after you've already forgiven me." His hoarse entreaty was filled with pain.

She met his grieving, abysmal eyes across the darkness, and cursed herself for letting them move her.

"I haven't forgiven you," she said. "I've admitted that I'm still in love with you. I've given in to that need. But that doesn't mean I've forgiven you."

"But you will when I tell you."

Unconvinced, Elise turned away from him and started out of the camper. Two jean-clad men with pistols strapped to the left sides of their chests waited beside the camper door, and when she saw them, she gasped.

"It's okay," he said. He tried to dispel his own uncomfortable feeling at the new men Cranston had sent. "Let's just go on in."

The men followed them into the house, where at least ten others, including Sam, sat in a conference over coffee and cigarettes that filled the room with a haze. Elise gave a dull glance over the men, one by one, wondering how dangerous they were and what they were all hiding from. Her breath caught when her eyes met those of Gary Rivers, the sergeant on the Vicksburg police force, who she had been involved with before Clint. Her mouth came open of its own accord. He had known. He had been involved. And when she had begged for his help after Clint's disappearance, he had lied. "For God's sake!" she mumbled on a broken voice. He had even asked her out a few months ago, when he had *known* that Clint was hiding somewhere waiting to get back to her. "Gary?" The word, in itself, was an accusation.

Clint's eyes hardened when he saw Rivers stand up and reluctantly look her in the eye. What was Cranston trying to pull? he wondered with outrage. Sending Elise's ex-boyfriend! Rivers had been involved at certain intervals throughout the ordeal, but even Cranston had enough sense not to put one under the "protection" of the other. Anybody could see the conflict of interest waving before them like an invisible banner.

"How are you, Elise?" The question came as calmly, as guilt-filled, as she expected. Clint heard the restrained emotion and the edge of tenderness, and wanted to deck him.

"I'm just great," she muttered sarcastically. Raising her chin, she turned to Sam, her eyes narrowed against any more surprises. "Where's Karen?"

"In the first bedroom on the right," he said. "She was dead to the world."

Elise shivered at the choice of words. "I want to see her."

"Go ahead," Sam said wearily, matching her defiant tone.

She looked at Clint, and with a brooding expression, he nodded that it was all right.

The room where Karen slept, like the rest of the house, was decorated in rustic neglect. It smelled of dust and staleness, and the oak floor was scuffed and scratched, and dirty probably from years of muddy hunters' boots tromping over it. But the bed looked inviting, and Karen lay curled up like a baby kitten.

Elise wanted to kill her. Sitting on the edge of the mattress, she shook her. "Karen, are you all right?"

Karen pulled the covers up over her head. "Geez, Elise. I'm asleep." She snuggled into a tighter ball.

Elise tried to wrestle the covers away from her. "Karen, wake up!"

"What is this?" Karen snapped. "Boot camp?"

With a sigh of long-suffering irritation, Elise shook her head. "Karen, we were just abducted and driven to some dusty rundown house out in the middle of nowhere after driving for hours. Doesn't that make you the least bit curious?"

Karen shook her head. "It makes me tired."

"Well, at least that aspect of my curiosity is satisfied. Obviously that man didn't hurt you."

"Sam's a pussycat," Karen mumbled.

"A pussycat? Karen, he packs a gun and he's dangerous."

Karen struggled to open her eyes, but only managed two slits. "Read my lips, Elise. He's a pussycat. The worst crime he's guilty of is singing off-key." She giggled into the pillow. "And you should hear how he slaughters perfectly good lyrics. There ought to be a law."

Elise stared at her friend, her blue eyes luminous with tumult, and wondered if Karen was right. "Then you think they're on the right side of the law?"

"Could be."

Karen's state of noncommitment was exasperating, but for a moment Elise turned the possibility over in her mind.

"My father's in on it," Elise mumbled finally.

Karen's head came up in a sudden exhibition of interest. "Your dad?"

"All along," Elise said. "Clint just told me."

Karen threaded her fingers absently through her tousled blond hair. "Wow. What else did he tell you?"

"Nothing yet. I wanted to see you first."

"Well, go beat it out of him. What are you doing talking to me?"

Elise focused on the comforter beneath her, and traced a pattern on it with her fingertip. "Gary Rivers is out there too."

"Gary?" Karen sat all the way up this time,

shaking her head as if to clear the fog. "Wait a minute. Gary was in on it?"

Elise nodded. "It's all getting so big, and so complicated. I think I'm afraid to know."

"Well, it couldn't be as bad as it seems," Karen said. "It never is." She yawned and gave Elise her sleepy assessment. "So how'd it go back in that camper? I gave you up for dead when I quit hearing the yelling."

"We stopped yelling for a while," she said softly. "All it took was the reality of a knife scar in his side."

"A knife?" Karen swallowed. She was fully awake now. "As in sharp pointed thing that does serious damage when thrust into flesh?"

Elise nodded.

"Go get details, Elise, before my imagination gets as carried away as yours."

Reluctantly, Elise stood up and looked back down at her friend. "How's your knee? Need aspirin or anything?"

"Sam already got me some," Karen said, settling back under her covers. "I'm just going to sleep through this whole thing. Wake me up when we get to the good part."

The good part, Elise thought as she left the room and started back up the hall. *And what would that be?* Lowered voices from the living room beckoned her, and softening her footsteps, she stepped toward the door and listened.

"But he's dead." Clint's voice came clear and angry over the others.

"Did you tell anyone? Your boss, or a friend?"

"Do you think I'm stupid?" Clint returned. "I got my job back on my own merit and my history of accomplishments. I didn't have to spill my guts."

"Then obviously Jake told someone. Maybe that's why he died. Maybe they didn't think they could trust him because he waited so long to tell them."

"There was no way I could have known. Cranston seemed sure that the man was so wrapped up in playing 'good citizen who made a few minor mistakes' that he wouldn't try for revenge," Clint said. "He was too scared to make a wrong move, Cranston assured us. How was I supposed to know that he was wrong?"

"You could have listened to us." She recognized Gary's voice—deep, accusing. "We told you it was too soon to go back there."

"What was I supposed to do? Just watch my life go by like it's some bad dream? For all I know it could have been eight more months before I was able to go back."

"Well, your impatience brought the DA's daughter into the line of fire, and he's not happy about that."

"And you think I am? She's going to be my wife. I would never have dragged her into this intentionally."

"But you did, nonetheless."

She heard Clint's footsteps, heavy, irate.

"You're not fooling anybody, Rivers," Clint blurted. "Your concern for her has nothing to do with the fact that she's the DA's daughter."

137

"Well, at least I *have* some semblance of concern! Not like you, dragging her into this mess just to satisfy your sex drive."

Something fell over and crashed angrily onto the floor, and the noise of a scuffle ensued.

"Stop it, Clint," Sam shouted. "This isn't helping anything. We've got to stand together. This guy was sent here to help protect you."

"Somebody'll need to protect *him* if he doesn't keep his filthy mouth shut!" Clint thundered. "Why did Cranston send him here, anyway?"

"He trusts him," Sam said. "There's no room here for grudges."

Tension seemed to float in the air like a lethal gas ready to explode with the lighting of a match.

She heard Clint stalk across the room. "I want to make something clear to you, Rivers," Clint said in the low vibrato of fury. "I've had about as much of this crap as I can take. This is *my* life. I'm the pawn here, not you. None of this was my idea, and I didn't ask for it. If it weren't for me, Cranston wouldn't even have a case. I've had it up to here with putting a hold on my life and waiting to be called to the stand and wondering who's going to jump out of the bushes next and who I can trust and if the woman I love is going to die because of something that I never even wanted to see!"

Elise caught her breath and struggled to follow his words.

"I'll stay here with you for as long as it takes to get out of this, but I'm not going to take any more of your accusations. I could disappear right now and Givanti would go free, and you know it."

Givanti! Elise stepped into the doorway and locked astonished eyes with Clint's black, piercing eyes. He relaxed his embattled stance a bit at the sight of her. He was the mystery witness in the Givanti trial that her father had been prosecuting. He wasn't a criminal. He wasn't a kidnapper. He was *trying* to be a hero.

But one didn't have to know all the details to see that Givanti must have people after him. And it was her father's fault that Clint was the primary target for every thug in the area. *Her father's fault.* No wonder he wasn't trying the case himself. Her relationship with Clint presented a conflict of interest.

"Now, if you'll excuse me, gentlemen," Clint said sarcastically, "I need to talk to my fiancée. I'm sure she has a lot of questions, and she's as entitled to answers as anyone. We're going outside."

Two men got up to follow after Clint, and he ground his teeth together and shoved his hand through his hair. "I'd like to be alone."

"That's impossible," Rivers said with finality.

"Then keep your distance," Clint warned. "Let me explain this to her without making her feel like there's a sniper waiting to fire at us."

Elise shuddered, and Clint grimaced at the regretful image he'd just used. Before things got worse, he led her outside.

The sky was star-studded, and the crescent moon hung overhead like a painting. Crickets chirped a deceitful song of peace, and wind whispered through the leaves and in her hair, cooling the burning feeling of horror shooting through her. The two men waited a few yards behind them, eyes alert and hands at their sides, as if they fully expected to be needed.

"You're the star witness in the Givanti case," Elise said in a low murmur before Clint had the chance to begin. "I've figured that out. What I don't know is how."

Clint dropped wearily to a tall patch of grass and leaned back on his elbows. "Remember Jake Calloway?"

"The co-op student," Elise said. She recalled the handsome young man with blue eyes and shaggy brown hair, and the ambitious spirit they'd all admired. She hadn't seen him in months. He'd been at Mississippi State University this semester, she assumed.

"The last day I saw you I found a vial of cocaine in his lab coat and I went to see him to confront him about it. Only it happened that I wound up witnessing a drug deal and a murder."

"Jake?" The word was spoken on a wave of incredulity.

"No, Givanti. He killed Anderson and didn't know Jake had anyone in the house. Jake helped him hide the body. I went to tell your father, and when I went home that night, Jake was waiting with his knife. Luckily, when your father realized I was gone, he sent squad cars to my house to make sure I was safe, and it frightened Jake off before he could finish what he'd started."

140

Everything good in life seemed to be slowly fading with phantasmic uncertainty. "He tried to kill you? That sweet kid?"

"That sweet kid was in some big-time trouble. I suspect he's spent the last few months looking for me. We gambled on his not telling anyone about me because it would have endangered his life for making a mistake."

She dropped to her knees on the ground and riveted her eyes on a blade of grass. "Is he the one who sent me that letter?"

"No. Jake's dead. He was found after an explosion in some abandoned building. When I got the word, I figured I was safe. Since I was going to be called to the stand pretty soon, anyway, I insisted on going on back home. I wanted to see you."

"But you didn't count on Jake having told anyone about your connection?"

"No. And I was wrong."

Elise turned toward the wind and set her hand on her forehead. She was beginning to feel sick. Sick with the terror that Clint had faced for so long. Sick with the months of emptiness that shouldn't have occurred. Sick with fatigue and hunger and a fear that was beginning to be chronic. "So what now?" she asked in a dull cadence. "Does my father intend to hide you out here forever?"

"No. Just until I testify."

Fury rose in Elise's neck, threatening to stifle her words, burning her throat. "And then what? Doesn't he think they'll get revenge? Doesn't he know that they won't let you just walk out of that

141

courtroom, if they let you walk in in the first place?"

"Givanti wasn't The Godfather, Elise. He was just a stupid, small-town politician who got in trouble with his gambling debts and figured this was an easy way to get himself in the black. We aren't talking about the Mafia. We aren't even talking about a man who's particularly smart. His cohorts weren't even that loyal to him, because they've made all kinds of deals with your father in exchange for information on how they got the cocaine into the country and things like that. If I can get him put away, I really believe we'll be safe."

A gust of wind whipped Elise's hair into her face, and she slapped it away. "What about the note, Clint? What about the bomb at the place you were staying? Obviously he's not going to sit still and let you do this!"

Clint didn't answer. Instead, he looked at her as if the instances she'd named were small events he chose to forget. Elise wanted to scream. "I can't believe my father would put you in this position. I can't believe he'd use your life to buy a conviction!"

"He isn't using me, Elise," Clint said. His eyes were intransigent, and full of conviction. "He's kept me alive when I couldn't have myself."

Her lips compressed into taut lines, full of contempt and despair. "And he made me think you just didn't love me, that you got cold feet, that I wasn't enough for you. All the time I was seeing

142

guilt in his eyes when I thought it was sympathy. It just makes me sick!"

Clint's expression was soft now, no longer containing the bitterness she'd witnessed earlier.

"He did the best thing for you. If you'd known, you would have run after me. Everything would have started to look suspicious, and what Givanti and his men didn't know, they would have figured out. I disappeared, and then Jake did, and then if you had, it wouldn't have taken a genius . . ."

"That's no excuse!" Elise bellowed. "That's absolutely no excuse for lying to me! Or putting your life in jeopardy. I'll never forgive him for that!" She caught her breath on a sob and fought back tears.

Clint tore a weed out of the ground and looked down at it. "Elise, I know it's hard for you. But you'll get past this confusion and you'll see that neither your father or I had a choice. We did exactly what we had to do. We betrayed you, but you know that you would have done the same thing in our place."

Elise swung around, her hair lashing into her face with the force. "How do you know that?"

"Because you're as strong as I am."

Elise threw up her hands, then let them fall heavily to her sides in helpless denial. "You and Karen, you both think I'm some kind of rock. You both keep talking about how strong I am." She tapped her chest. "Look at me, Clint. I've been shaking for two days. I'm inside out. I'm numb. You call that strength?"

143

"You're dealing with it, Elise."

"Dealing with it? If you think I'm dealing with anything you don't know me very well. I'm tired of coping, Clint. I'm tired of trying to hold myself together by a thread. I feel like I'm hanging on the side of a building, about to fall."

Clint's voice cut across the night and into Elise's heart. "I know the feeling."

Elise leaned toward him, her blue eyes wide and desperate, full of unshed tears. "Then let's leave. Let's just blow it all off and go somewhere else. You don't have to go through with this. My father cannot make you risk your life."

"I'm not doing this for your father. I'm doing it for me. For my conscience."

"And what about me? I lose the one man I love because some stupid kid got into the wrong crowd? Does that make sense, Clint?" When he didn't answer, she closed her eyes and tried to massage the pain from her temples. "Why did you have to go over there, Clint? Why did you get involved with Jake? It was none of your business!"

"You liked him too, Elise. We thought he was our friend. He needed guidance and help. How could I have known I was going at the wrong time?"

"The wrong time? That's like saying Hiroshima was the wrong city. It changed our *lives,* Clint. It might have cost our lives, and it's not over yet." She took his face in her hands, and thought how it was the dearest face she'd ever

144

known, and how close she'd come to never seeing it again. "Don't do it, Clint."

"I have to." His voice cracked, and she heard the glitch in his breath.

"Not if you love me," she said. "If you really love me, you won't be a hero. You'll give it up and let the professionals worry about it."

Clint took her arms, and his eyebrows arched, emphasizing the new lines on his forehead that spoke of the hard life he'd been leading since he left her. "Baby, you know I love you. But I have to do this. Otherwise this whole eight months was a waste."

"It's a waste, anyway, Clint!" she shouted. "And it's going to keep being a waste until you put an end to it."

"There won't be an end until I testify."

"There won't be an end until they *kill* you!" she shouted, shaking away from him. "And me too. If you loved me, you wouldn't drag me through this hell. You'd see that there are other ways."

"You're blackmailing me, Elise," he said quietly.

She bit her lip and swallowed back a sob. It was true; she was blackmailing him. But it was the only weapon she had. "Call it whatever you want to, Clint. But as long as you plan to go through with this, I don't want to have anything to do with you. I can't stand it. I've mourned for you once. I don't want to do it again."

"Elise, you're all I've got. Don't—"

"I have to, Clint." She stood up and started

toward the house. "I'm going to bed. I'll sleep in Karen's room."

And as emotion threatened to overpower her, Elise walked past the two guards and left Clint watching after her, devastated, regretful, and absolutely unyielding.

"It's never as bad as it looks, pal," Sam said an hour later when he came out to Clint, still sitting sullenly in the grass that swayed around him like bacchic spirits mocking his plight. Sam had a folded lawn chair in each hand, and the dot of light from his cigarette intensified as he inhaled.

Clint didn't answer. As close as he was to Sam, he didn't want to talk. But that had never swayed Sam before.

"The grass is always greener on the other side," Sam said, slumping into his chair and offering Clint the other. He watched as Clint got up, dusted off his jeans, and plopped down.

"One in the hand is worth two in the bush." The line was delivered with great somberness. Clint gave Sam an annoyed glance, but still chose not to speak.

"Yeah," Sam said on a yawn. "Every cloud has a silver lining. That's the kind of guy I am."

Clint issued a barely audible moan. "I keep reminding myself that I should feel lucky that you didn't put a tune to those little bits of wisdom."

Sam laughed, simultaneously blowing out a puff of smoke. "I figured you were miserable enough."

Clint shrugged. "Miserable. Is that what they

call it?" He looked into the wind, letting it ruffle his hair. "You know, Sam, life was no bed of roses when I was a kid. But I was pretty proud that I made something of myself, anyway. You feel better about yourself when you make it on your own, with obstacles behind you that most people never have to face." He stopped and swallowed, and contemplated the stars. "Adversity always makes us stronger, and I keep telling myself that. But lately it seems that I've run out of positive sides. Everything keeps blowing up in my face. The rules of the game seem to keep changing, and I can't keep up with them."

Sam thumped his ashes and cocked his head, listening. That was the thing about Sam, Clint thought. He could listen like no one else.

"I don't know if I ever told you," Clint went on, "but my dad was a construction worker. Died when I was five. Fell from a building he was working on. My mother had to support my kid brother and me after that, and it wasn't easy. And then when my brother got sick . . ." His voice trailed off at the helpless memory of the little boy dying, and his mother's grief. Swallowing, he continued, his soft voice doing battle with the rustle of the warm wind. "Well, things were never the same after that. But we did the very best that we could. She always taught me a sense of honor, a sense of doing what you believe is right, a sense of holding your head up even when it hurts." He stopped and sighed. "Now she's gone, too, and I can't tell black from white. Ah, Sam. Am I doing the right thing?"

"What do you think?" As usual, Sam's answer was nonjudgmental, noncommittal.

"I think it's tearing Elise up. And it's tearing me up. I never expected it to hurt quite this much."

"What did you expect? For it to be easy?"

"No." Clint leaned forward, propping his elbows on his knees and staring up toward the house. Was Elise sleeping, or was she lying awake in torment like he was? Was she crying? "I just never expected to have to make such a sacrifice. My whole life is just dangling. I thought going back for Elise would get it back into focus. I thought . . ."

"That she'd understand? Give her a break. She's probably scared to death. She'll come around."

"Will she?" Clint held Sam's eyes for an eternal moment, seeing ghosts instead of a friend's concern. "What if she's changed? What if eight months has dulled some of her feeling? What if we can't get it back? What if that Rivers bastard in there thinks he's going to win her back on his mission of mercy? Her champion, her . . ."

"And what if you're full of crap? Anybody can look at that woman and tell she's quivering inside over you. What if all this has made it stronger? That's the thing about living on the edge. You don't take things for granted. If anybody knows that, I do."

Clint heaved a sigh. "I wouldn't even mind being taken for granted, if I could keep from dragging her through hell. All I want is my job, a

148

family, a home where the most exciting thing that ever happens is that the washing machine breaks down. I'm not like you. I don't thrive on adventure."

Sam uttered a high, disbelieving laugh. An owl hooted in the distance, joining in the mirthless exchange. "Is that how you see me? As some clown who thrives on adrenaline? Forget it, Jessup. That picture you just painted looks pretty good to me too. Danger is not all it's cracked up to be."

"It's the sacrifices, Sam," Clint sighed. "The damnable sacrifices. And the wondering . . . wondering whether it's worth it. Whether you've sacrificed more than you intended. Whether you should run like hell while you still can." He looked at Sam, bracing himself for an argument, hating himself for needing one.

But Sam only dropped his cigarette on the ground, and stomped it out with his foot, exhaling with a sibilant breath. "Nobody can tell you what to do, buddy. It's your life and your choice. I don't know what to tell you. I don't even know what I'd do in your place. All I know is that you have enough sense and enough courage to do the right thing, whatever that is. Maybe it's running off and taking Elise with you, so you can start that family without constantly looking over your shoulder. Maybe it's seeing this through to the end. I don't know."

Clint looked at his hands, hands that were shaking, hands that had known blood, and guns, and the soft, sweet feel of a woman's face. "Either way, a lot of people get hurt. If I do what Elise wants and skip out, I've wasted eight months of your life, and all the time Cranston and Breard have put in . . ."

"Hey, pal. Stop right there," Sam said, pointing at him. "I was doing my job. If I hadn't been doing it for you, I'd have been doing it for someone else. Don't hang this on me or Cranston. It's your ball game. If you want to declare it a forfeit, it's your choice."

Clint leaned back in his chair, propping his nape on the aluminum back. Was it really his choice? Could he really live with himself if he abandoned it now? And if he didn't, could he bear to live without Elise?

Even if she could live without him. After all, she had done well enough for the past eight months. *What do you want, Jessup?* he asked himself. Did he want to know that she had shriveled up and nearly died with grieving over him? Or did he simply want to know that there hadn't been a moment when she'd turned to someone else. Someone like Gary Rivers.

Someone she might turn to again.

CHAPTER TEN

Karen slept like the dead, but it was a luxury that didn't come easily for Elise. She lay on top of the covers in the big bed next to her friend and stared at the high ceiling, wishing for the luxury of privacy so she could weep without being heard. She couldn't get over what she'd learned tonight. The danger, the lies, the betrayal . . .

And she had thought Gary Rivers was her friend. He seemed to care months ago when she had begged him to help her find Clint. With sympathy and a listening ear, he had pretended to "pull strings" to find Clint. And when he had come to her, backing up everyone else's story about Clint's cold feet, he had seemed honestly sorry. Why hadn't she seen it? Why hadn't she suspected him of knowing where Clint was all along? She remembered the night he had shown up on her doorstep, summoning all his charm when he'd asked her to have dinner with him. He'd played on her memories of their past relationship, but he hadn't been able to get past her memories of Clint. She had turned him down gently, despite Karen's protests. Had Karen been in on it too? Had everyone in her life betrayed her? Had that entire chapter of her life been nothing more than a sadistic lie, a lie supervised by her father?

She closed her eyes and cursed herself. Eric Cranston had always been good at manufacturing lies, even when she was a child. She had forgiven him for them when she got older, for he had made it up to her many times over. But she had never forgotten the feeling of utter betrayal by both her parents—first her mother when her father, unable to explain the concept of death to a six-year-old child, had told her that her mother had "gone away" and was never coming back. "But she didn't tell me good-bye," she had cried. And she had turned to the steaks marinating in the refrigerator as proof that her father was mistaken. Her mother had prepared three of them for dinner that night. Didn't that mean she would return?

After weeks of close protection and virtual isolation from anyone who could have broken the news, she had overheard her father admit that his wife had died in a sudden car accident. And when the news had sunk in, she had felt the second betrayal. How could her father have lied to her? How could he have believed that it was better for her to think that her mother had abandoned her by choice than to mourn honestly, like a little girl struck with the unfairness of the world?

This was the same thing, she thought miserably. The exact same thing. Had he sent Gary to her to get her mind off Clint, whose life he counted as over? Her father had thought it better to make her believe that Clint had simply stopped loving her than to tell her that he was sending him into hiding and that he might never make it out. *Might never make it out!* The thought played over and over in her mind, making her stomach cramp and her head throb.

She sat up on the bed and looked helplessly around the dark room. She wasn't going to sleep until this tension found an outlet. She needed some air, some peace, some release.

Quietly, she got up and put on her shoes. She would go out, she decided. She would slip out of the house and try to breathe. And if she could find a place, she would try to jog off some of the knots stagnating in her muscles.

The air was hot and muggy, and the wind skipping across the ground was unsympathetic. It was the kind of night that foreboded disaster, the kind of night that seemed predestined. Elise looked up into the opaque sky and wondered if anyone out there really cared about the sufferings of Clint or her. She searched herself and found that she still believed there was. *Faith is just a flimsy piece of self-betrayal,* she had told Clint. But had she really believed it? Hadn't she always had faith in him, deep down inside her somewhere?

But it was a selective faith. She believed in Clint's love for her but not in his ability to make the right choice. "Damn," she whispered brokenly. She started to walk aimlessly, then broke into a run, despite the fact that she still wore jeans and shoes not meant for the sport. Her feet pounded the dust and dirt beneath her, and humidity encompassed her, but she ran the length of the house, and her breathing came in dry, sobbing gulps.

Suddenly, as she rounded the side of the house, she heard a clicking sound and a violently uttered, "Freeze!"

She did as she was told, and before she could protest she was slung against the house, and a man's hands were sliding over her body, searching deftly for a weapon. "Please," she said, cursing herself for being careless when she'd known better. "Please . . ."

Immediately the frisking stopped, and she turned around to look into Sam's steely eyes. "Lady, are you crazy?" he grated. "I could have killed you! I thought you were . . ."

"One of the bad guys?" she bit out with mocking false bravado.

He let her go, but kept the gun trained on her. "As far as I'm concerned, that's what you are. You've done a lot more to hurt Clint than Givanti or Jake or anybody else who's wanted to do him in."

Elise bristled. "Oh yeah? And I suppose you've made him think you're his loyal friend, guarding him from harm. But you aren't his friend, you're his prison warden!"

Sam only stared at her, his steely eyes hardening into narrow slits.

Feeling she had the edge, Elise added, "And you can get that gun out of my face."

Sam dropped it to his side. "Where were you going, anyway? Trying to pull another vanishing act?"

"No," she answered, wanting to hit him. "I was tense. Frustrated. I couldn't sleep, so I was trying to run some of it off. I didn't expect anybody to jump out of the shadows and pull a gun on me. Don't you ever sleep?"

"I *was* sleeping," he said. "But I sleep light. And I heard you out here sneaking around. You're just lucky it was me."

"Excuse me while I go count my blessings."

She started to walk away, but Sam grabbed her arm roughly and stopped her. "You want to count your blessings, lady? Let me help you. Clint Jessup is alive. He's healthy. He loves you, God knows why. And he's finally reached a point where there may be an end to this crap. You need more blessings?" he bit out, eyes blazing. "How about this? You're alive, and other than a little 'frustration' that sends you flying out in the night like you're invincible, you're unscathed. I'd say you have a lot to feel lucky about."

Elise lifted her chin defiantly. "Get your hands off of me."

"Gladly," Sam grated, letting her go with a slight shove. "As long as we have an understanding."

"What understanding?"

"No more careless midnight jogs. Clint has enough on his shoulders without having to stop

155

everything and mourn for his woman. And I'd hate to dig your grave."

"I'm deeply moved."

"Don't be," he said. "It's Clint's need for you I care about. Other than that, you could run into a rainstorm of bullets for all I care. I feel compelled to keep you alive for his sake."

"Karen couldn't be more wrong about you," she mumbled, starting back to the house.

Sam caught up to her in two steps. "What did you say?"

"She called you a pussycat. Said singing off-key was your only offense. I'll tell her she was mistaken."

A wistful look passed over Sam's gray eyes, and he swallowed. "Yeah. You do that."

And then he passed her and went into the house, as if he was the one who had been wronged.

Elise stood staring at the door for a moment. Finally, out of fear instead of fatigue, she stepped inside the screened porch and started for her room.

Gary Rivers was leaning against the door that led from the porch into the house. Elise only glared at him and brushed past him, for they had nothing to say to each other. She'd had as much machismo as she could stomach for one night.

"Wake up, Elise!"

Elise cracked open her eyes and saw that the sun had come up to paint pink-orange hues on the warped walls of the old structure. "What is

156

it?" It seemed as if she had just closed her eyes and her run-in with Sam had been only a moment ago.

Karen was sitting up straight in bed, her eyes flashing with exuberance and excitement. "I want to know what happened last night. Did Clint tell you what's going on?"

Elise pulled upright and shook her head, trying to allay the hung over feeling after her nightmarish night. "Yeah."

"Well, don't keep me in suspense."

Rolling her eyes, Elise slid off the bed and stumbled toward the bag that Karen had packed hastily when Clint had decided to take them. If she just had a cup of coffee, she thought. No, forget coffee, she told herself. A toothbrush and a hairbrush ought to do for now. Then she could tell Karen what she had learned. "I . . . toothbrush . . ." she mumbled.

She unzipped the bag and reached inside. Her hand closed around something small and rectangular, and she pulled it out. "A novel?" she asked with disbelief. "Clint told you to pack absolute necessities, and you packed a novel?"

Karen shrugged. "I couldn't think. I just grabbed what I thought was important. I didn't know how long we'd be gone, or if we'd have a TV . . ."

Elise reached in again. "Dental floss?"

"I hate getting food stuck in my teeth."

"Well, I certainly see how that could be at the top of your critical list." Dreading what she'd find next, she stuck her hand back in. "Your leo-

157

tard? Karen, what did you think they were going to do with us? Aerobics?"

Karen moaned. "I'm sorry. I just grabbed whatever I could find. I got some of your stuff too."

"I hope so," Elise said. She reached in again and drew out a bag of pistachios. "Pistachios! Now that's more like it. And who says you can't think on your feet?"

Karen gave a smirk. "There really are toothbrushes in there. And a change of clothes for each of us. And a little mascara in case the need arises."

"Why would the need arise?"

"Don't you want to look your best for Clint?"

Elise lowered her eyes and looked at the pistachios in her lap. "Karen, Clint's in a lot of danger. He's the witness for the Givanti trial, and all these men are here to keep him alive until he testifies."

"Sam too?"

"Yes." Her voice was raw. "We're all in danger, but Clint is the one they're after. They want to stop him, and I'm afraid they will."

Karen lifted her chin and swallowed, looking at the wall with rounded eyes.

"You like Sam, don't you?"

"He's . . . he seems like a decent person," Karen said.

Elise refrained from telling her about the volatile confrontation she'd had with him last night. "He's liable to get hurt, too, if Clint does. And so are we."

158

A distant look glossed Karen's eyes, and she pulled off of the bed and went to the dusty mirror to straighten her hair. "I wonder if they have coffee in there," she said in a hollow voice.

Her evasion of the subject didn't surprise Elise at all. "Karen, I've got to convince Clint not to testify. That's the only answer."

It was as if Karen didn't hear. "Then Sam's a cop?"

Elise stifled the urge to call him a lurking lunatic with a license to own a gun. "As far as I know. He's been protecting Clint."

"So if someone shoots, it's his job to stop the bullet?" Her face reddened with the words, and she stared, expressionless, into the mirror.

"Something like that, I guess."

Karen started for the door. "I'll see if they have coffee," she said quietly.

Dumbfounded, Elise watched her turn her back and simply walk away.

"Do you always look like this in the mornings?" Sam's voice, gravelly from too little sleep, came from behind Karen as she poured herself some coffee.

Karen wasn't sure where her smile came from, but when she turned around she couldn't dismiss the one wreathing her face. "Is that a compliment or an insult?"

He gave a lopsided grin. "Don't want to commit myself," he said.

She sipped her coffee and looked at his sleepy eyes and the blue Ole Miss T-shirt he wore with his holster strapped across his chest as if it were a part of him. "So you're a cop, huh?"

"Yeah, but you aren't really surprised, are you?"

Karen gave a slight shrug. "I don't know. I sort of had you figured for an underworld spy of some sort."

"Did you really? And did you think that your abduction was a matter of international security?"

Karen raised her brows and pushed her flaxen hair behind her ears. "It might have been. I thought maybe I'd uncovered a criminal ring in one of the pictures I took at the park, and I was being chased for the negatives, and it was your job to make sure that I, and my film, were safe."

His chuckle came from deep in his throat. "You watch a lot of television, do you?"

Her eyes widened flirtatiously, conveying that he was right, as she sipped her coffee.

"So where's that top secret film?" he asked.

Karen frowned. "That was the only catch to my theory. I forgot it."

She surveyed the laugh lines crinkling his eyes, eyes that had lived hard and fast and told her things about him that she doubted he would ever have said himself. As he stood before her they were waking up, becoming brighter, more alert. "You must not need much sleep."

"Not as much as you, obviously."

She looked at the swirl of her coffee, remembering the gentle way he had tucked her in the night before.

"How's your knee?"

She bent it for him. "Fine. A little sore, but I'll survive. I may limp for the rest of my life, but—"

The screen door slammed, and Sam swung around to see Clint leaving the house. "I have to follow him," he said, cutting her off.

Karen followed Sam to the door and looked out over his shoulder. "There are guards out there with him."

"Yeah," Sam said distantly. "I like to stick close, though, just in case."

Karen gave a heavy sigh and stepped off the porch. Sam ambled ahead of her to a fallen log, just slowly enough to offer her an invitation. "It's big enough for two," he said.

Karen cupped her coffee in her hands and sat down next to him, where they had a clear view of Clint walking aimlessly across the ungroomed grounds. "So you've been guarding him like this for all these months?"

"Eight months," he specified. He pulled a pack of cigarettes out of a pocket and lit one up.

"Don't you get tired of it?"

"Not as tired as he does," he said, exhaling a stream of smoke. "Besides, we've gotten to be tight friends, and I don't have many of those. That roommate of yours is giving him hell, you know. And he doesn't need any more of that."

The wind whipped Karen's hair away from her face, and she looked at Clint. "Elise has been through it too. If anyone's seen that, I have."

"So you've sort of been doing for her what I've

161

been doing for Clint all this time," Sam said. "Protecting her."

Karen considered the comparison a moment. "Not really. Protection is not my forte. I'm a believer in accepting things the way they are. If I've done anything for Elise, I've kept her from dwelling on things."

She watched Clint start toward an old building on the property, a barn or garage of some sort, and the two guards followed at a good distance behind him.

"Well, she needs to dwell on this," Sam said. "Clint needs her right now. That's why we took the chance of letting him go back in the first place. It was a mistake, but at least it got her here. And now she's pulling this self-righteous stuff on him."

"She's not self-righteous," Karen quipped. "She's scared to death for him."

"Well, she should be," Sam said, sending a chill down her bones that she very much wanted to dispel. "But turning her back on him and confusing him with petty ultimatums isn't going to solve things."

"And what will? Letting him get shot to death as an example for anyone else who decides to cross Givanti?" She felt her face reddening, and her hands began to tremble. She'd never wanted to talk to him about this. She hadn't even wanted to think about it.

"He won't as long as I'm here." Sam's voice was broodingly earnest.

"And what about after? You won't be there

162

forever. After the trial, when they decide to get revenge, is anyone going to be there to protect him then? And how long? Indefinitely? Even a good friend can't take that kind of responsibility."

"I thought you said protecting Elise wasn't your forte."

"It isn't. Understanding her comes a bit easier, though. She doesn't see an end to this. Do you?"

Sam dropped his cigarette, and ground it into the dirt with his heel. "I wouldn't be here if I didn't."

From the porch, Elise watched Clint walking around like a man carrying a great burden. Two guards flanked him, obviously lending more stiffness to his demeanor. She fought the urge to go after him, to tell him she was just confused, that she desperately wanted him safe, and that the only thing she was certain of was her love for him. But if she loved him, she had to stop him. And running after him wouldn't do it.

She watched as he threw a rock into the distance, his back rippling beneath his T-shirt as he reared back to throw another. He had been working out in these eight months, she told herself. His shoulders seemed much broader than they had before, and she had recognized the new, corded power in his biceps and chest when he'd made love to her last night. Sliding down the wall of the house until she sat on the rotting planks, she closed her eyes. Why hadn't she made that last longer? Why hadn't she had more time to

163

experience his arms around her, his body fitting over hers with weight that made her heart sprint, his softly chiseled mouth playing games with hers?

Clint dropped to the grass, his back to her, and rubbed his hands roughly through his hair. Her heart melted and left a void in its wake. Across the yard, she met Sam's eyes—cold, accusing, dull. Look what you're doing to him, they said. And suddenly she knew that Sam was right.

Swallowing back her misgivings, she got up and stepped down the four steps off the porch, and let the wind finger-play her hair as she stood watching him. He stared out at the trees that surrounded him, those broad shoulders slumped in hopeless defeat. And she knew he was thinking, *there's loss either way, there's no way to win* . . .

. . . *Absolutely no way.* Clint raked both hands through his hair and dropped his head. Why had he expected Elise to alleviate some of the pain and dread? Why had he expected her to understand what he had to do? And why did those damnable guards have to breathe down his neck?

Two soft hands, laced with the faint hint of a tremor, closed over his shoulders. Elise's hands.

He looked up at her, saw the despair and the turmoil in her eyes, and wanted to wipe it away. But he feared she saw it in him as well. A soft sigh escaped his lips as he took her hands. His brows arched in grateful relief, and he moved her hands to his face. She had come to him. She was

164

here. Oh God, she wasn't going to hold back after all.

She stooped on her knees behind him and pressed her mouth to his shoulder. "I love you, Clint," she whispered. "I love you. And I don't want to lose you again."

"You won't," he assured her. He pulled her around to face him, and cupped her chin with his hand. "I'm right here. Let's just take one day at a time."

"I can't think that way," Elise told him. "I can't live that way."

"But it's just for a little while longer. Your father will send for me any day now, and I'll go on that stand . . ."

"Don't do it, Clint." Her face reddened with the words, and her eyes welled up, breaking Clint's heart and blurring his mind.

"I have to."

Elise bit her lip and looked over Clint's shoulder. "Oh, can't you get rid of those guards for a minute? Can't we talk without someone hearing every word?" Her voice was straining toward the breaking point, but he knew she wouldn't let herself break until she was in private. She had always been strong that way, but today he didn't want her to have to be strong.

"That barn's private," he whispered. "We could go in there. It isn't the cleanest place in the world, but—"

With a shaky hand, Elise wiped at her tears. "Will they let us?"

Clint pulled her up and started toward the

barn, calling back over his shoulder, "We'll be in the barn. We have to talk. ALONE."

The two guards looked at each other, then nodded acquiescence. After all, what harm could there be in going into a decrepit barn?

The air smelled of old hay, rusty tools, and mildew, but the privacy was worth it. Elise turned to Clint in the dark room, lit only by one small window on either side of an empty hayloft. Elise's eyes held a glint of wildness, of frantic desperation, when she faced him. She took his arms, her hands trembling harder with the force of barren wishes. "Clint, I've been thinking. I could get Karen to help. She could say we were in the house or something, and we could slip out the window and take the camper. If we could get to the airport, I have my credit cards and we could get airline tickets. We'd be long gone before any of them caught up to us."

Clint shook his head slowly, and his hands came up to cup her elbows. "Baby, those people out there are not the bad guys. They're protecting us."

"Just long enough to get what they want out of you!" she blared. "Then they'll leave you at the mercy of anyone who wants you."

"It won't happen that way."

"How do you know? Can you give me guarantees?"

"You know I can't."

"Then come with me!" she shouted, shaking him. "I *can* give guarantees! I guarantee that if we leave we won't have to live like fugitives for

166

the rest of our lives! I guarantee that we won't have to be afraid of someone trying to kill us in our sleep!"

"It's not that way, Elise. Givanti's setup isn't that big. We'll go away after I testify, if you want. But not now. Not before."

Elise hugged herself and tucked her chin into her chest, trying desperately not to fall apart. "Clint, I'm begging you," she whispered, though she knew it was futile. "Please."

The word was issued on a choking sob, and her face was crimson with the force of her plea. Clint stepped toward her and took her in his arms, letting her cry against him like an orphaned child facing the destruction of the world.

And as he had several times over the last twenty-four hours, he wondered if he was, indeed, doing the right thing.

Karen and Sam stepped over branches and pushed aside bush limbs as they attempted a stroll on the wooded bluff surrounding the camp. Karen held a twig whose leaves she kept pulling off, letting them flutter to the ground. When Clint and Elise had disappeared into the barn, Sam had seemed willing to let it go at that, and he had brought her up here "to see what she was made of." Smiling to herself, she reflected how she had passed his "endurance test" if liking the woods was the criterion. "Maybe I'll come back here with my camera when this is all over," she said. "Want to come?"

Sam chuckled and ducked under the limb of a

young loblolly pine. "There are other places I'd rather go."

"Like where?" she asked.

"Anywhere but here, or the other place we've been hiding. Home has a nice ring to it." He turned back to her, leaning on the limb that reached between them. Laughter and deep thought fanned out from his eyes.

"But you said you didn't have a home."

"Not really. When you haven't seen your apartment in months it's a little hard to call it home." As if to change the subject, he looked back toward the camp. "Look at this," he said, his voice lowering to the pitch of a sigh. "We're up so high you can see the whole spread from here."

"If you wanted to, I guess," she said with an insouciant shrug. She dropped her bare twig and turned around, waving her hands in an all-encompassing gesture. "The beauty's behind us, though." She pointed to a platform up in a tree. "Is that where they sit when they deer hunt?" She turned back to Sam and saw his pensive gaze on her rather than the deer stand.

"Yeah," Sam said. "Want to go up?"

Karen bit her smile. "Are you sure it can hold us?"

Ducking back under his branch, Sam gave a soft laugh and took her hand, gesturing with the other. "Only one way to find out."

Never one to turn down a challenge, Karen started up the ladder, careful not to strain her sore knee. The platform was much stronger than

168

it looked, and she pulled onto it and waited for Sam.

With feline agility, Sam climbed up beside her. In the sunlight, reaching in fingerlike rays through the trees, she saw for the first time how tanned he was. His brown hair was brushed with streaks of blond that spoke of much time outdoors. She tried to picture him sunbathing, and giggled silently at the image she conjured of his bare chest with the untanned imprint of a gun. She had no idea why that struck her as funny, she realized suddenly. For the gun disturbed her too much to be laughed about.

"So what do you think?" he asked, sitting down next to her. Their arms brushed. Their faces were inches apart, and his breath smelled faintly of tobacco and coffee, and a warm scent that she had come to know as uniquely his own.

"About what?" His eyes seemed to grow darker the closer they moved to her.

"About the stand. Do you like it?"

She drew in a shallow breath and looked around her. The pine trees created a shelter overhead, a giant, green rooftop that cooled the sun's rays. Beneath them, blueberry bushes shared earth with dogwood, and younger pines rustled among them. "It's beautiful," she whispered. "Just beautiful."

Sam nodded agreement, but his soft, lambent gaze told her his opinion that the area's beauty was trapped elsewhere. "I like a woman who knows the value of a place like this."

Karen wet her lips. "I like a man who likes a

woman who knows the value . . ." Her voice trailed off as he wet his own lips and moved slowly closer.

Their eyes embraced for a moment, and she held her breath. He was going to kiss her, and every fiber within her stood at red alert. Her heart did a drumroll, and her stomach did a triple flip.

But he stopped before their lips met. "Did Elise tell you about our run-in last night?" he asked, almost as if it had some bearing on his intention to kiss her.

She shook her head. "What happened?"

"She thinks I'm a prison warden, and I think she's ungrateful. We were in strong agreement, however, about our mutual dislike of each other. I was sure she'd try to make you see what a miserable bastard I am."

Karen narrowed her eyes and wondered why Elise hadn't mentioned it. Probably because it wouldn't have mattered, she mused. Karen never was easily swayed once she made up her mind about people. "She didn't mention it. Just that you're a cop and you're in as much danger as Clint."

A look close to surprise skittered across his eyes, then settled into relief. He pulled back a fraction to look at her. "Doesn't that make you afraid to be around me?" he asked lightly.

Karen frowned. It was another test, she thought. It was almost as if he was searching for a reason for her not to get involved with him. And somehow, it mattered to her that she pass this one too. "Heck no," she said. "If there's going to be any danger, what better person could I be with than a cop? Not that I believe you could hurt a fly."

The flicker of a shadow fell over his expression. Suddenly, he withdrew, and she knew she had said the wrong thing. "Let's get down," he said, his tone reticent. "I need to get back."

The abruptness of his letting the magic drop surprised her, and made her the slightest bit angry. "Well, could you?"

Sam turned around to her at the ladder, his eyes hooded. "What? Hurt a fly? I've never had one pull a gun on me. I don't know." He expelled a quick breath and started down. "How the hell did we get on this subject, anyway?"

Confused, Karen gave a dejected shrug and followed him down. He seemed struck with something that drove him some mental distance away, and her brief surge of anger dwindled. When she was back on the ground again, she touched his arm. "You know, I didn't mean to—"

"Shhh," Sam's hand came up to silence her, and his brows knitted in an apprehensive frown. "Listen."

She did, but she didn't hear anything.

Sam took a few steps to the edge of the bluff and looked out over the barn. The two guards were playing cards on a broken stump, and nothing looked out of the ordinary.

Karen gasped when he drew his gun.

"Go back to the camp," he whispered. "Now. Hurry!"

"But what's—"

"Do what I say!" he whispered again.

Karen started back, looking over her shoulder every few steps to see what Sam was up to. She saw him take off on feet trained to be quiet around the bluff to the clearing behind the barn where Clint and Elise still were.

And then she saw what had changed his mood. A man sat in a grove of bushes, arm cocked back to throw something at the barn. She started to scream, but she heard Sam's voice shout, "FREEZE!" and then a gunshot.

And in the wake of the worst sound she'd ever heard in her life, came an even worse one. The sound of an explosion.

CHAPTER ELEVEN

A sound like the end of the world burst on Elise's ears and she screamed. The acrid smell of smoke wafted on the air from some source outside the barn, but Clint still stood before her, his hands trembling as he grabbed her against him in a gesture that spoke of terror and fierce protection. Quickly, he cracked the door open and looked out, and satisfied that no one waited in ambush, he pulled her out behind him.

The patch of grass where they had sat together just moments ago was burning, and two guards were extinguishing it. The rest of the men who occupied the camp, however, were gathered on the bluff overlooking the barn, squatting over something on the ground.

Elise saw Karen running toward the house, arms wrapped around her waist, a look of stifled horror on her face. "Karen!" she called, but her friend didn't answer. "Karen! What happened?"

Karen stopped, but didn't turn to Elise. "Sam . . . shot . . ." The words were barely audible, and Clint didn't wait to hear the rest. Vaulting toward the bluff, he pulled Elise behind him.

"It's Sam," he rasped in a panicky voice as they ran. "Sam was shot!"

But before the words could sink in, a shaky, familiar voice reached their ears singing "Let It Be."

Clint stopped running when he saw Sam standing on the outskirts of the group of men, his face as white as a colorless sky. His hands were shaking as they raked through his brown hair, but he managed a smile for the man for whom he had risked his life.

"You almost bought the farm, buddy," he said.

"Looks like you came close yourself. What happened?"

Sam indicated the man on the ground. "Had a grenade with your name on it. I just diverted his aim a little."

"You shot him?" Elise's question was hoarse and disbelieving.

Sam assessed her for a moment, his self-deprecating expression silencing her. "Yeah, I shot him," he bit out. "If I hadn't, you wouldn't be here to pass judgment."

Elise bit back her retort. All she knew was that a man was lying on the ground, probably dead, and they were searching his wallet, without much surprise or concern. She forced herself to look at the face, then gasped in surprise. He was young, probably a teenager, nineteen at the most, and he looked innocent and mischievous and a lot like someone she knew but couldn't place. Tears sprang to her eyes and choked her, and she looked away. "He's so young," she whispered. "Couldn't you have—?"

Sam's lips trembled with the strain. Setting his hands on jean-clad hips, he leaned toward her. "He had reared back to throw a grenade at the barn where you and Clint were inside. What do you think I should have done differently? *Talked* it out? Fired a warning shot? Run like hell? I did what the situation called for. I did my job."

"But he's just a kid." She knew it wasn't Sam's fault, and that she owed him her life. But the knowledge didn't make reality any easier to bear.

Gary Rivers sliced through her thoughts when he looked up, his own face whiter than Elise had ever seen it. He flashed the man's driver's license at Clint. "Name's Calloway," he said. "Mark Calloway. Did Jake have a brother?"

Clint shook his head. "I don't know. He never said."

"He did," Elise said. "He mentioned him to me once."

Gary stood up and handed the wallet to another officer, then set his hands on his hips and looked pensively down at the body, as if he, too, were struck with the youth of the young man.

"He must have come to get revenge for his brother's death," Clint said.

Gary nodded his head slowly. "And failed."

Elise looked up at the note so close to regret in his voice, but quickly shook it off. "And if he knows where we are," Sam added, "then someone else must too."

175

"But Clint didn't kill Jake," Elise blurted, the significance of what had just happened finally becoming apparent to her. Had someone really tried to kill them? Had someone been watching them enter the barn, and subsequently tried to destroy it?

"Are you sure he was alone?" Clint's words shot through her like missiles.

"Some of the men are still combing the woods, but my guess is that he was alone," Gary said. "If there's anyone else out there, they won't get away."

Elise felt a sudden surge of nausea, and she leaned into Clint, whose arms tightened around her. "Then we have to leave again?" His voice held dread couched in acceptance.

"No choice." Sam patted Clint's shoulder. "The only problem is how to get out of here without being followed. But time is crucial. If we can just keep you out of trouble for the next couple of days, we'll be home free."

Elise closed her eyes and tried to calm her whirling terror and anger, reminding herself that emotional outbursts rarely accomplished much. "I assume you'll be letting my father know of this latest development. Am I right?"

"Of course," Rivers said. "He has to be kept abreast of—"

"Then I want to speak to him." The words grated out through clenched teeth. "You take me with you when you call and you let me speak to him."

"Elise." Clint's voice was admonishingly low,

and it infuriated Elise even more. "It won't change anything—"

Her hands were shaking, and her legs barely supported her. "It might! If he knew how stupid this was. If he knew how we felt about all this—"

"*We* don't feel that way," Clint insisted gently. "You feel that it's a mistake, and I don't. I'm going through with what I started, baby. It's the right thing."

"The right thing? Being killed for the sake of one man? Is that the right thing, Clint?"

Until he reached up to wipe back her tears, she hadn't known she was crying. "Just stand behind me," he whispered. "That's all I ask."

"For what?" she spat out. "So that I can catch you when you're full of bullet holes? So I can see that you have a proper burial? Get Sam to stand behind you! He seems to believe in this lunacy."

She threw a haughty glance toward Sam, almost expecting a saucy retort, but he didn't seem to hear. His eyes were trained on the camp, on the porch of the rickety old house, to the woman sitting on the floor with mixed disappointment and denial in her pallid expression.

"I need you." Clint's words came as a shaky plea.

"Why, Clint?" She jerked away from him, and wadded the roots of her hair. "Have you become numb to the excitement, the adventure, after all these months? Do you need one more element of danger to keep the suspense going?"

"Elise, don't. You don't mean any of this."

"Oh, I mean it," she cried, looking back at

Sam. His sterling eyes were not singing anymore, and his face was momentarily unguarded. For a moment, she felt sorry for him. She felt sorry for all of them. She wanted to scream, she wanted to collapse in a heap of tears, she wanted to run as far as her feet would carry her, she wanted to fling herself against Clint and hold him as if it might be their last day together. But all she managed to do was start walking down the bluff, toward the friend who seemed to need help in dealing with what she had just witnessed, and away from the man who needed more help in dealing with what he had witnessed months ago.

When she reached the porch, she leaned against a rotting column and looked down at Karen. If Karen would only cry, she thought, she would know what to do for her. It was only this stony facade that she didn't know how to handle. Did she want to be left alone, or did she desperately need her company? "You all right?" she whispered.

Karen nodded.

"We'll be leaving now," Elise told her, wiping a shaky finger under her eyes. "Seems like there's no place safe to hide, though."

"Who . . . who was it?" The question almost surprised Elise, for it wasn't denial.

"Jake Calloway's brother. He was about to throw a grenade on the barn while Clint and I were inside."

Karen nodded quickly and swallowed, and she focused on a chair across from her, her eyes unblinking, as if she feared they would shatter into tears if she did. "I saw," she said. "He had reared back to throw it, and Sam said, 'freeze.' And then there was the shot. So loud that it seemed to go right through me. And for a minute I thought Sam was hit. And then the explosion, and the fire, and I didn't know if he'd gotten you and Clint or not."

"We're fine. Everyone's fine."

Karen drew a deep, quivery breath. "Why does everyone have to be a hero?"

Elise couldn't answer. Instead she turned away and looked back toward the bluff.

CHAPTER TWELVE

Although she knew the possibility existed that they could be blown away in ten seconds flat if the right person managed to follow them in their unmarked, bulletproof station wagons, Elise was numb to the fear. Clint's silence and his pensive perusal of the trees whisking by on the edge of the narrow road made her want to scream. Gary Rivers, who drove the car, was equally quiet, and Karen hadn't quite pulled out of her depression yet. Sam wasn't even singing, she realized, and for the first time, she wished he would. Instead, he watched the windows, as if he expected a passing car to open fire on them all.

They hadn't been driving long when Gary pulled into a rest stop to call Elise's father. "Come on, Elise," he said when he climbed out of the car.

Clint's hand clamped over her wrist. "She's not going anywhere with you, Rivers."

"The lady wants to talk to her father," Gary sneered. "So she's coming with me."

Clint turned to her. "I don't want you to go. It's too dangerous."

"I'm a cop, remember?" Gary's reminder was directed toward Elise. "Besides, I have a stake in your safety myself. Why do you think your father sent me?"

Clint's hold on Elise's hand tightened.

"Let me go, Clint," she said softly. "I want to talk to my father. It'll be okay. Gary won't let anything happen to me."

Her assurance stung Clint worse than a slap across the face. His eyes narrowed with pain. "You trust him more than you trust me?"

"It's not a matter of trusting one of you over the other," she said. "I just want to talk to my father."

Clint relaxed his grip resignedly, and she got out of the car. Rivers's triumphant grin filled Clint's eyes with murderous passion. "Tough luck, Jessup," he said, too low for Elise to hear, before he slammed the door.

Elise could feel Clint's eyes on her as they walked toward the small building. She shrugged off Gary's attempt to set his arm on her shoulders.

"What are you so mad at me about?" he asked when they rounded the building, out of sight of the others, and found the pay phone.

"Get my father on the phone," she clipped. "I didn't come out here to talk to you."

Blowing out a frustrated breath, Gary slipped in a quarter and dialed the number. She listened as he got orders from her father, then explained that she was waiting to talk to him. Then, with an appeasing pat on her shoulder, Gary handed her the phone.

"Hi, honey." Her father's endearment only infuriated her, and she bit her lip.

"Dad, I want you to put a stop to this madness right now. I don't want Clint to testify. I want Breard to find some other way to win your godforsaken case."

Cranston cleared his throat. "Honey, you don't understand. We don't even have a body. All we have is Clint's word. There *is* no case without him."

"Then drop it!" she said. "It's not worth his life. Someone just tried to kill him."

"I hear you were in that barn too." His voice was tighter than before.

"Yes, Dad. Think about that. You've gone to such lengths to protect me for the past eight months. If I get killed right beside Clint, all those lies were wasted. All that energy trying to look sympathetic. All the satisfaction for letting me think, again, that I wasn't worthy of being loved! If you can't see Clint as a human being, then think about me. Enough people have died, Dad."

"We won't let anyone else die," he said with little conviction.

"You can't stop it as long as this trial is going on!" she rasped. "You're murdering him a little bit at a time! I don't understand how you can do it!"

"You're under a lot of strain, honey. You're nervous, and I don't blame you."

182

"I'm scared," she said. "More than I've ever been."

"So am I," he admitted. "Especially now that you're there. If I could stop it now, I would in a minute. But I can't."

"All that power," she mocked. She pressed her forehead against the phone mounted on the wall and squeezed her eyes shut. "All that power and you can't save the man I want to marry. It's ironic that justice over one man's life is probably going to cost so many more. Or is it justice you're really after, Dad? Maybe it's not. Maybe it's just a little glory. A little more recognition. A little more power."

"Elise . . ."

She couldn't bear to hear his denial, or his declaration of his love for her, or his pleading that it was out of his hands. So she dropped the phone in its cradle and kept her forehead pressed against it. There was no one she could turn to to make Clint stop. No one who could be trusted.

"It'll be all right, Elise," Gary said. He set his hands on her shoulders and pulled her back against him.

"Get your hands off of me," she warned. "I'm about as happy with you right now as I am with my father. You betrayed me too. I thought I could trust you."

"You *can* trust me," he said. He turned her around to face him and bent his head down to hers.

She met his eyes defiantly. "No, I can't. You were the first person I turned to. And you lied to

183

me." She gave a mirthless laugh as the memories came back to her. "You even tried to get things started up between us again. When Clint was fighting for his life!"

Gary's face hardened. "If it weren't for him, we'd still be together. You can't blame me for trying to get back something that he took from me to begin with."

"He didn't take me from you!" she retorted. "It just wasn't working out with us, Gary. We didn't love each other."

"I loved you," he blurted. His hands tightened on her shoulders, and he pulled her closer.

"Let go of me," she said cautiously. "Gary . . ."

"We were good together," he whispered. "We could be again, Elise. Your father knew it. That's why he let me come. That's why I was one of the only officers he kept informed on what was happening, so I could step in if I had to. He always liked me better than Clint."

"That's not true," she said, but suddenly she wasn't certain.

"It is," he insisted. "And he knew that I could protect you better than Clint or any of those others. Because I still care for you."

"Let go of me." Her voice wobbled. "Gary, this is not—"

His mouth came down on hers, not forcefully, but not gently either. And before she had her arm reared back to slap him, she heard running footsteps and the sound of fist confronting flesh. Gary let her go as he was slung to the side, and she saw

Clint lunge for him, grasping him around the throat, throwing him to the ground and straddling him with death in his eyes.

"Clint, stop!" she shouted, and Sam tore around the corner.

"Jessup! Rivers!" He tried to pull Clint off of him, but met with resistance.

"You scum!" Clint railed. "If I ever catch you touching her again—"

Sam jerked him loose, and Gary scrambled to his feet, blood clotting at the corner of his mouth. "I look forward to seeing you dead, Jessup!" he spat. "And I probably won't have to wait long. Cranston's calling you to the stand tomorrow!"

The angry statement hit Clint like ice water, and he dropped his hands to his sides. Elise caught her breath and took Clint's arm, but he jerked it from her and started back toward the car, leaving her feeling accused for something she'd never done.

She and Clint didn't speak during the long ride to their next hiding place, even though Sam was now driving their car and Gary was in another, but she couldn't help wondering what went through his mind. Not doubts about her relationship with Gary, she hoped. And not anger and judgment. He knew her better than that—or he should. But hadn't they both changed enough not to completely trust the other anymore? She shook off the thought and looked out the window at the Natchez Trace whizzing by again. He needed to be concentrating on staying alive tomorrow, when Gary's cruel premonition of his death would be tested. He needed to try to relax.

Her throat knotted as she watched his fingers dig into his thigh, watched the other hand finger the gold chain at his neck, watched the subtle nervous habit of him shaking his foot, and heard the intermingling of shallow and deep breathing that told her of his frustration and dread. He stared, unseeing, out the windows, shutting out her quiet rejection of this morning, shutting out tomorrow, shutting out yesterday. She reached for his hand, but he recoiled and a muscle in his temple twitched, revealing the anger he held in check. A shiver went up her spine as she withdrew her hand and vowed to clear the air as soon as they were alone.

When they reached the new hiding place that her father had arranged for them, Elise didn't notice that it was on the Ross Barnett Reservoir, about an hour's drive from where Clint would be taken to court. She wasn't aware of the subtle wealth sanded into the grain of the luxurious weekend home on the water, and it didn't yet cross her mind that it probably belonged to a friend in a high place. The only thing that plagued her mind was the look of despair in Clint's shadowy eyes, and she intended to set things straight before he even got into the house.

The door slammed behind him when they were all out of the car, and Clint went to the trunk to get his suitcase and started toward the house.

"Clint," she said, catching up to him. "Clint, we have to talk."

If anything, he sped up, but she followed beside him, and saw the angry huff of breath and the tight way he closed his eyes.

"Clint, what happened back there was not my fault. You know it wasn't."

His throat convulsed as he reached the front door, and he opened it and stepped inside. Elise was getting angry.

"Clint, stop and look at me. We have to talk."

Setting his mouth in a tighter, grimmer line, he started up the stairs. He was going to blame her, she realized with alarm and the initial sting of fury. He was going to ignore her as if she weren't even there. "Clint, don't you do it!" she grated from the bottom of the stairs. "Don't you dare shut me out!"

Gritting his teeth, Clint flung his suitcase to the top floor, its loud crash resounding throughout the house as he swung around to face her. "Why the hell not, Elise?" he shouted. "Isn't that what you've been doing to me ever since you laid eyes on me three days ago?"

"No!" she said. "I was confused and afraid."

"And you don't think I was?" Color climbed his neck and seeped under the stubble darkening his jaw, and a cord in his neck swelled. He held the banister and leaned toward her. "You think I like playing these games with you, Elise? You think I like wondering what mood you're going to be in from one minute to the next? Whether you're going to love me or detest me? Whether you're going to support me and stand behind me or fall into some jackass's arms?"

"That's not fair!"

"Fair?" A dry, chilling laugh tumbled out of Clint's tight throat, his mirthless eyes slashing her heart. And then he turned and started back up the stairs, and retrieved the suitcase that had opened with the impact of its fall. "Damn right it's not fair, Elise," he said over his shoulder before he disappeared into one of the bedrooms. "Damn right."

Elise dropped her face against the banister. She wasn't strong enough for this, she thought. She was crumbling, and it was affecting him. But she didn't know what to do about it.

He came back to the head of the stairs a moment later, clad in a pair of red jogging shorts and a white tank top that revealed the straining definition in his arms and chest and the stiff set of his broad shoulders. His skin glowed with a bronze hue, but his face was pale, strained, distant. He didn't even acknowledge that she still stood there as he started for the door.

"Are you going to run?" she asked in a flat, metallic voice.

"Obviously."

She swallowed and started up the stairs. "I'll change and run with you."

"Forget it, Elise. I want to run alone," he said.

Elise stopped and waited as he slammed the front door, and felt herself melting into a throbbing mass of nothing. The feeling made her angry. He was not going to do that to her, she resolved. *He is not going to shut me out when he needs me the most!* Setting her mouth in a stiff

188

line, she ran up the stairs and searched the five bedrooms for the one with his suitcase. When she found it, she riffled through it and pulled out a pair of his shorts. *So they're a little big,* she thought, wriggling out of her jeans and slipping the shorts on. They were better than anything Karen had brought for her.

She glanced out the window, and saw that Clint was already beating a trail around the large house, and that most of the cops that had come with them were pacing around the grounds in feigned exploration, when in reality they were probably ready to pull their guns and open fire at the least little crackle in the trees.

Karen was coming up when she bolted down the stairs, and she stopped and grabbed her friend's arm. "Can I wear your tennis shoes?"

"I'm wearing them," Karen said.

Elise rolled her eyes as if the observation was irrelevant. "Karen, it's important. I have to go run with Clint."

Brushing her fingers through her hair and sweeping it behind her ears, Karen eyed Elise's feet. "Well, at least you're wearing socks . . ."

"Karen, please!"

"All right." Expelling a long-suffering sigh, Karen set down the duffel bags she had carried in and jerked off her shoes.

"Thanks," Elise said, and slipped them on as fast as she could. Then she rushed out, and waited for Clint to come around before she joined him.

She started to run beside him, though his pace

was faster than she was used to. "If you think you're going to get rid of me this easy, you're in for a surprise," she huffed next to him. "I'm not leaving your side again. For any reason."

Clint didn't answer, but he sped up, as if doing so would cause her to fall back. But summoning all the strength she had built up over her years of jogging, she managed to keep his pace, at least for a while.

After several laps without slowing down, however, Elise realized that Clint was running with fury, with rage, with the need to purge himself of his pain, and the intent to hurt himself worse than anyone else could. His arms and legs were red, as blood pumped furiously through his body.

"Clint, slow down," she panted. "Please. I can't—"

"Then stop, Elise!" he said between breaths. "Nobody's making you run with me."

"I'm not leaving your side!" she shouted. "I'll pass out first."

He kept running and she followed, though every muscle in her body rejected another step.

"Clint, I love you." She wiped the perspiration out of her eyes and forced herself to keep up with him. "I'm sorry I hurt you."

He kept pounding the packed dirt, remaining a wall of numbness that she feared she could not penetrate.

Tears escaped her eyes and mingled with the perspiration. "Clint, please. I can't do this much longer."

"You can stop anytime you want to," Clint rasped.

She stumbled, and he slowed a degree and looked over his shoulder. The simple gesture gave her hope and enough strength to catch up to him again.

"Not on your life," she said furiously. "I'm going to keep this up as long as you do, Clint. I'm going to collapse with you!"

"Leave me alone, Elise!" He bolted ahead of her, picking up speed again, and she saw blood on the heel of his shoe, but still he ran. She followed as fast as she could for several laps, but finally he stumbled and lost his momentum. Seizing the opportunity, she lunged forward. He tried to pick up his speed, breathing furiously, but she reached out and grabbed the back of his T-shirt.

"Stop, Clint," she cried. "Please . . ."

He tried to shake free, but she caught his arm. The force made him trip again, slowing him enough for her to throw her arms around his waist. And then, with all the strength she possessed, she flung herself to the ground, pulling him with her.

He caught her before they hit the dirt, and threw himself beneath her to prevent her injury. His breath came in gasps, his pulse was runaway, and his arms trembled around her. The pain on her face shook him back to reality, and her rampant tears mingled with the sweat on his face as he held her.

"I love you," she grated through her teeth. "I

love you no matter what you do to me or yourself. And you can't run from that."

His shoulders quaked, and he buried his face in her neck and held her, coughing as his lungs screamed for oxygen. The pink of his skin drained to a pallid gray, suddenly matching hers, and she wanted to lie there and comfort him until their breathing settled. But he pulled up and coaxed her to her feet. "Get up, baby," he told her. "Come on, get up. We have to walk."

Wiping at the perspiration on his face with the back of his hand, he draped his arm across her shoulder and pulled her beside him. They walked at a brisk pace for a lap, then two more, slowing until they were able to stop. And when their breath returned to normal and their hearts were no longer threatening to resign, he pulled her against him and again dropped his face into her shoulder. "I can't do it without you," he admitted in a forlorn whisper. "Not any of it."

"You won't have to," she returned, in spite of what it would mean. "Not any of it."

Then he pulled her into the house, up the steps, and into the bedroom he had chosen. She sat him on the bed, and carefully worked his jogging shoe off of the injured foot, then the other. One tear dropped onto the bloody spot as she looked at it, but Clint cupped her chin and brought her face to his. His kiss was gentle, grateful, as tender as all his love. "The foot will heal," he whispered. "The heart needs a little more care."

And Elise knew that she had no choice but to mend the heart that needed her.

* * *

It was a miracle, that love in her eyes, Clint thought with a melting heart. He had wanted to run himself to oblivion, to numb every thought and feeling in his soul after seeing another man kissing her, but she had stopped him. And amazingly, his emotions seemed keener instead of more blunted now that he knew she would not turn her back on him again. He had known the kiss was against her will; he had heard every word she'd exchanged with Gary since Sam had let him out of the car. But it still hurt.

He blinked back the mist in his eyes and swallowed the emotion stopping his voice. Her mouth moved to his neck, making him shiver at her touch, but her sudden warmth and softness took every ounce of fatigue and stiffness from his muscles. Soft lips, wet lips, moved to the indention below his throat, down the hair-sprinkled chest to his damp shirt, and back up his neck. His hands slid up her sides, and she covered his mouth with hers again, her tongue inciting anguish that burned and swelled and yearned. Her thighs brushed against him, and he moved his hands down her back and over her hips, pulling the legs tighter against his groin. A slow, sensuous, side-to-side massage began as she swayed to some unheard melody, and he inched his hands back up the tight, smooth legs, beneath the baggy cloth of her shorts. A gentle sigh swept from her throat, and he breathed it in, enchanted by her spell.

"There hasn't been enough love," she said

softly against his lips. "Too much fear. Too much fight."

"No fighting now," he whispered on a husky breath.

He stood up then, and she followed him, capturing his lips and ravaging his warmth, drawing the pain from the base of his soul so that she could nurse it and put it to rest. Her power over his pain was instant, yet the healing ritual lingered for long moments. His breath was deep and ragged, and his heart thudded against her breast, setting a primitive rhythm that played havoc in her heart. This was escape, he thought on a wave of bursting bliss. This was what he'd needed.

Her breasts grew firm and sharp beneath her damp blouse, crushing against him, driving him mad. He moved his hands to them, cupping their fullness with tingling palms, framing their swell, teasing their tips with his thumbs. She moaned, and he felt the vibration in her chest. Her breath came wilder against his face, and their tongues grew bolder as they swirled with urgency. Her hands slid from his chest down his back, to the hard, flat buttocks, bracing him for her hips as they ground against him.

"The door," he groaned in a broken voice. "It's open."

She kissed him again, as if she didn't hear, moving in ways that drove him mad and almost made him forget the noise and activity right outside their door. His own hands left her breasts and glided behind her, lending greater pressure to

194

the tight hips as they lured him to the bounds of thoughtlessness. He heard footsteps on the stairs, voices in another room, a television, . . . and her fragmented breath against his ear. Closing his arms around her waist, he lifted her. Backing her against the door, he closed it, then let her slide down, sandwiched between him and the door. She was trembling in his arms, and he could feel her bare breasts beneath her blouse crushed against him, the hard, straining nipples driving him to distraction. His fingers fumbled with the buttons of her blouse, baring the valley between her breasts, exciting him into fierce discomfort. When he came to the last one, he unveiled her, sliding his work-roughened hands over the bare, hot flesh, savoring the tautness, the sharp, circular tips, the tantalizing heave of them. The blouse fell to the floor, and he braced her with an arm on her back as he dipped his mouth to one alabaster mound set in contrast to her golden tan. He reveled in her gasp of delight, and caught one peak with his teeth, suckling and teasing and swirling with his tongue until she arched her throat and moaned.

She struggled to pull his shirt over his head, and in moments it covered hers on the floor. They stood facing each other for a moment, sharp, aroused nipples crushed against his hard chest, thick, male arousal pressed against straining female need. Her eyes were like a blue sky signifying the end of a solitary sentence, as enticing as light at the edge of a cave. He loved her more than he loved the sun or the sky, for he knew there would never be darkness as long as he had those eyes as his beacons.

Her lips moved to his chest, to the crisp hair curling there, then to his own brown circles, one at a time, biting and making his body burst to life while she twisted his gold chain on a finger.

His lips fused and melded on hers, the kiss crossing the threshold of passionate excitement and becoming plundering and desperate. Her fingers feathered down his stomach, and he sucked in a breath and waited. They dipped in the waistband of his shorts, teasing miserably, torturing sweetly as he rumbled out a deep, aching moan.

Slowly, with trembling hands, she pushed the cloth over his hips, snapping his control and reveling in his crazed desire. Then they were stepping from their clothes, and her hands were moving over him, and he was marveling at the tight silk of her skin, the moist warmth inside her, the sweet shiver of her breath against his ear.

He entered her with all the restraint he had in his soul and all the gentleness he had in reserve. She clung to him, gasping.

In moments they were on the floor. His embrace made her tremble, his strength made her weak. So she clung with all her might, reeling to the same heights as he, bursting in a million fiery, crumbling bits until he pulled her back together and held her.

And when they lay anchored, satiated and exhausted in each other's arms, he moved her to the bed. She lay entangled with him, and suddenly the fear and danger outside the door struck her again, threatening to rob her of another night, another moment with Clint. She stroked his face and looked into his eyes with eyes, again, full of tears. "Clint, I'm scared. I'm so scared."

His solid, unyielding embrace gave her reassurance. "Everything will turn out fine. Because I love you. And you love me. And God is not cruel enough to take that from us."

But as Clint closed his eyes and settled into relaxed sleep that only her love could have induced, Elise had the hollow feeling that someone else was.

CHAPTER THIRTEEN

"Pretty night," Karen said as she came upon Sam sitting pensively in the dark outside the door with a glowing cigarette in his mouth.

"Pretty lady," Sam returned, smiling. "But I thought you were avoiding me for dear life after what you saw this morning."

"You were the one who didn't come to dinner," she pointed out softly.

He smiled and took the cigarette out of his mouth, and dropped the ashes at his feet. "You call slapping a piece of bologna between two slices of bread *dinner?*"

Karen shrugged. "We've all got to eat."

"Yeah, well." He put the cigarette back in his mouth and narrowed his eyes as he inhaled. "Guess I wasn't hungry."

Karen sat down on the bench next to him and braced her elbows on her knees. Cupping her chin in her hand, she looked out over the dark water rippling in the breeze. Tree frogs exchanged mating calls in the distance, accompanied by chirping crickets and an occasional splash of an acrobatic fish. Overhead, the stars shone clearly, and the air was cool, lacking the usual southern spring humidity. The atmosphere gave one the deceptive feeling of permanency, and though she knew it was deceptive, Karen clung to it. Fear was something that erected barriers, and she had no time for those. "What I saw this morning shook me," she admitted finally. "It made it all real. It made your job real, and that gun you wear, and that enemy I'd been hearing about but hadn't really cared much about."

Sam tipped back his chair, leaned his head back against the wall, and looked at her, the humor in his eyes gone. "You saw me shoot a man. I didn't want you to see that."

Karen swallowed, but she kept her eyes locked with his. "I really didn't think you were capable of such a thing," she said. But in her eyes there was no accusation. Just a deep, gnawing need to understand.

Sam dropped his cigarette and stomped it out. "We do what we have to do, Karen. There's nothing that says we have to like it or feel good about it. I had a gut instinct and I listened to it."

She nodded and sat erect, leaning her own head back. "On one hand, I was awed. If not for you, Clint and Elise would be dead. You saved their lives single-handedly. You're very good at what you do."

"And on the other hand?"

Though they were only inches apart, that distance seemed much too far. And at the same time, she had never felt closer to or more in tune with anyone. "And on the other hand, I didn't want to believe you had pulled that trigger."

"Why?" His voice came softly, like a caress.

"Guess I wanted to believe you were an innocent. Mysterious, maybe, but pure and untainted."

"But I mean, why did you want to believe that?" he asked. "Even when you thought I was some criminal trying to kidnap you, you didn't really seem afraid of me. It was as if you knew more about me than I had told you, even then."

Karen looked into those silver eyes that mirrored her confusion and her tenderness, and she thought how obvious it was that he was a good man. If he could only see himself that way, she thought, he would understand her certainty. There would be no question about her faith in his sense of right.

"I had a gut instinct and I listened to it," she echoed quietly.

He held her gaze for a segment of forever. "Has it changed?" he asked, finally. "Am I some tainted, evil man who stalks danger and frightens you now?"

A soul-deep sigh tore from her lungs, and she managed a soft smile. "If only you were," she whispered. "If only you were."

Their lips met in tentative offering, and Karen was awed at the softness of lips that she had been tasting in her fantasies. He shifted in his chair and touched her arm, such a simple gesture, but its tenderness devastated her. Slowly, she parted her lips beneath his. He found warm entrance, and explored with a sweet gentleness that touched her heart. Had she seen the violence and the tenderness in the same man, or was one just an image her heart had conjured up to protect her from the other?

The kiss ended, but Sam did not pull back. He looked at her with eyes that had found the gold hidden away at the end of his rainbow. He pushed her flaxen hair away from her eyes, and let his fingertips sculpt the crest of her cheekbone and the delicate slant of her jaw. "I don't know who sent you to me," he whispered against her lips. "But I'm glad you're here."

"So am I," she whispered, startled at the honesty of her emotions. "So am I."

Elise awoke with a start as a sound intruded on her slumber. Clint was gone, and she felt cold, and alone, and afraid. Wakefulness slowly pushed aside sleepiness, and she sat up and listened. The ordinary sound of the shower running in the adjoining bathroom settled her fears.

But it did not soothe her loneliness. She pulled out of bed and saw the bloody shoe lying on the floor, and wished she had done more for Clint's foot than put a Band-Aid on it. Was that what she had done with his life? Had she cured the immediate symptom of frustration and anger by promising to stand beside him? And what would be the end result? Would he be killed tomorrow because she hadn't succeeded in changing his mind?

So little time, she thought, as tears welled in

her eyes. Too little time to waste fighting about something that could not be changed. Clint would go through with this whether she wanted him to or not, because he believed it was right. And how could she be worthy of a man like that if she didn't stand behind him? She took a deep breath and thought about tomorrow. She would go to court with him, and hold onto him until they called him to the stand. And somehow her being there would make him invincible. It had to.

The bathroom door opened, releasing a cloud of warm, soap-scented steam, and Clint came out, a towel swathed around his waist and another draped over his shoulders. His gold chain gleamed against the damp curls of his chest, and his black hair was ruffled and wet, the sexiest, most treasured sight Elise had ever seen. He smiled when he saw that she was awake. "I'll never get used to seeing you look at me that way," he whispered. "I keep thinking I'm dreaming."

A twinkle of pain fleeted through her pale eyes. They *were* dreaming, and reality would intrude much too soon. Clint sat down on the rumpled sheets, one leg bent under him and the other on the floor. He bent over and reached under the bed for a box of his belongings, slid it out, and pulled out a smaller box.

"What is that?" Elise asked quietly. He smiled at her, all glowing and beautiful in the lamplight, and dropped a kiss on her lips. Then he opened the box, revealing a stack of papers covered with his handwriting.

202

"Your manuscript?" she questioned. "The book on sedimentation you said you wrote?"

He shook his head. "There was no book. I kept thinking there would be. But every time I sat down to write, I thought of all the things I wanted to say to you. And so I did. On paper, I told you everything I felt. It's like a journal. It was my only link to you." He breathed a great sigh and handed the box to her. "In a way, it kept you with me. It kept me sane. I want you to have it now, if you want it."

She took it, smoothing her fingertips across the ink and the page that testified to Clint's love, to the months of separation, to the fear and pain he suffered, and to the fact that he'd kept her in his mind as well as his heart.

"We can't get those eight months back, Elise, but this might help to fill them in. And the next time we're apart, it will hold us together again."

Somehow it sounded like a good-bye, but she told herself that he needed her to be strong. No more tears, she thought. There was too little time left. She would cling to the man who sat before her, and concentrate on the night's reprieve they had been granted. And if the day came for him to be torn away from her again, she would turn gratefully to the soul he had written down and handed her in a cardboard box. Then she would grieve and regret and hate.

But not before. Not before.

Reaching out, she hooked his gold chain with a finger and drew him closer. He leaned forward and set his hand on her shoulder, watched the play of moonlight from the window against the naked flesh, and the sensuous veil of shadow cast by his hand moving down her arm. He feathered his hand back up her arm and nestled it against her neck, then up through her silk-rich hair. And then he softly touched her face, the perfect cheekbone, the delicate chin, the soft slope of her nose. His lips pressed against one temple, then trailed to an eyelid, down her face, and finally to her mournful lips.

Outside the window, oak leaves rustled against the house, their lamentation stealing into Elise's heart, adding urgency to the kiss that warmed and ignited her. She moved her arms around Clint's neck and slid the loosely draped towel off of his shoulders. He peeled away the sheets that covered her nakedness, and his hands slid to her soft back as he lowered her to the pillow.

There were no words exchanged. No vows of love that time could distort someday. No whispered pleas for some far-off forever. Forever was tonight. Forever was the weight of his body over hers. It was the feel of rough hands sliding over satin flesh. The feel of soft hands gliding over crisp-curled hair. It was the thrill of desire growing against her aching core, and fulfillment only a towel's breadth away.

She bent one leg to cradle him, and he removed the towel. Adrenaline pulsed through her, as he moved inside and withdrew. His retreat incited a moment of agony, soothed only by the full thrust that made her gasp and arch beneath him.

He rolled beneath her and lifted his head, capturing one swelling breast. A husky moan issued from her throat as she moved above him and took his mouth.

The constellations smiled outside their window, each conflagration they created paling the one before, the dimmest of which still outshone the lonely stars. Their ardor reached above life, beyond defeated dreams. And it became a treasure that could not be taken . . . despite what tomorrow would bring.

But when rational, practical thoughts intruded once more, sleep wouldn't come for Elise, though it came for Clint. Elise lay on her side and gazed at the gentle, yet strong man beside her, sleeping deeply as if there wasn't the danger that his next moment of life might be snatched from him. Had she loved him enough? Had she loved him too much? Should she have held back and continued trying to make him succumb to her wishes? No, she told herself. That would only have made him more frustrated and tense, but it wouldn't have changed his mind. And he needed all his wits about him for what he would face tomorrow.

Tomorrow. Would it be the end of their nightmare, or merely a new chapter? What if Sam and Clint were wrong about Givanti's circle? What if it was bigger than they thought? What if it reached farther? What if . . . ?

Closing her eyes, she covered her forehead with her wrist. One thing at a time, she told herself. Just see him through the night, and be there while he needs you tomorrow, and believe that there is an end to the terror. Just push through one moment at a time, for tomorrow would come too soon, she reminded herself.

The men sat around the breakfast table the next morning sipping their coffee quietly, nibbling at their food with a noticeable lack of appetite, a marked difference to the other meals they had devoured in the last two days. Karen, pale and drawn, sat across from Elise next to Sam, who hummed softly. Elise hadn't known him long, but she had been around him enough to know that his singing often signified his anxiety.

Clint sat with his arm draped across the back of Elise's chair, his ankle crossed over his knee, in a stance that made him look at ease, but Elise knew better. She had helped him dress in his suit this morning, and had seen the distant, too accepting look in his eyes, and felt the rigid set of his muscles. And he had been quiet. Much too quiet.

One by one, the men left the table to go and prepare for the hazardous trip to court. Clint sat still, gazing into his coffee cup. When they were, at last, alone, Elise set her shaking hand over his. "We'll be all right, Clint," she whispered. "I'll be with you, and . . ."

"You can't go," Clint cut in, his eyes luminous with dread over telling her. "You have to stay here."

Elise's blue eyes filled with alarm, and she drew back her hand. "No. I'm going with you."

Clint shook his head firmly. "It's been decided, baby. It's too dangerous. You'll be safer here."

"You promised," she blurted, tears springing to her eyes, tears she had vowed not to cry. "Clint, you said that you wouldn't leave me again, that we would be together, that . . ."

He set down his foot and leaned toward her. "Elise, you know this is different. It can't be avoided."

Elise stiffened as he set his hands on her shoulders. "You can't keep me away," she forced out, determined not to cry. "I have to go with you."

"It's too dangerous."

"That's why I have to go!" she shouted. "If you're in danger, I want to be with you. We can survive it if we're together. And if you don't, I don't want to either!"

Clint caught his breath and pulled her against him, holding her with his eyes squeezed shut, as if it could keep out her terror and her reasoning. "I know that feeling," he whispered into her hair. "I do. But your father has left strict orders that you are not to come to the courtroom. And I agree with him."

Elise was trembling. "That's because my father knows that you'll be killed! If he's willing to let you get killed for his case, then he'll have to let me be too."

Clint pulled her back and took a deep, ragged breath. "I'm sorry, baby."

"No!" Elise jerked out of his arms and stood up. "They can't make me stay!" She bolted out of the kitchen, and approached each officer she

207

could find, but no one would help her. Sam seemed to understand her quandary, but he remained firm on the stand they had all taken.

It wasn't the finality of the decision that shook her, she realized when she tried to force herself to think clearly. It was the implication behind it. The implication that Clint would be hurt, and that she was not to be around when he was. She looked at Sam, and set her hands on her hips, struggling with the tears brimming. "I want you to tell me how you can be sure that someone won't blow him up before he even gets into that courtroom."

Sam looked at Clint with eyes that said he *couldn't* be sure. "If he gets blown up, so will I."

"Oh, that's comforting!" she said, throwing up her hands. "And to think I've been so concerned!"

Sam sighed roughly. "I meant that I'm not going to leave his side until he's on the stand. I'm a good cop, Elise. And Clint's a good friend."

Elise turned back to Clint, the fight draining from her. "Clint, please . . ."

Clint pulled her against his chest and walked her into the vacant living room. "I need your strength, Elise," he whispered, kissing the top of her head. "I need to know that you're back here waiting for me. That you'll marry me when I get back."

She looked up at him, as if he didn't know how much he was asking. Strength was such a rare commodity for her lately. His black eyes hid a wealth of emotion—more than most people know in a lifetime—and yet he seemed to cope so well.

"You will come back, won't you? And it'll all be over then?" She wouldn't think about afterward. If they could just get through this part . . .

"I'll be back," he assured her. "When do you want to get married?"

"We should have done it yesterday," she said. "We should have done it the first day you came back for me. We should have done it eight months ago."

"We can do it the day I come back, if your father can pull some strings."

Her eyes blanched to the color of frost. "I don't want my father to be a part of it."

"He will be a part of it," Clint said. "I want you to forgive him for this. He did the right thing."

"He put your life in danger. He's *still* putting your life in danger."

"He did the best he could, and he will continue to."

She straightened the knot in Clint's tie, and tried not to cry. "Let's not talk about him," she managed to say. "Let's talk about our honeymoon. Where will we go when this nightmare is over?"

"How about home?" he asked. "We could find a house and buy it, and move in and not come out for a few weeks. The locks and dams can wait. I want to relax with you, and make love with you without feeling that it could be our last time. I

209

want to hear you laugh again, and I want to see that smile creep back into those beautiful blue eyes."

"Come back to me and you will." Her voice broke with the promise, and a tear escaped to roll down her cheek. "Come back to me, Clint."

"I'll be back."

Someone cleared his throat from the doorway, and they both looked up. Gary Rivers leaned smugly against the jamb, watching them with disdain. "Sorry to interrupt this touching little scene," he said. "But I believe Clint has an appointment."

Slowly, as if he were being called to the execution chamber, Clint let go of Elise.

"Don't worry about her," Gary said. "I promise to take good care of her."

Clint's eyes whiplashed across the room. "What did you say?"

"You heard me," Gary said, his brown eyes challenging. "While you're in court being a hero, I plan to make sure that nothing happens to Elise."

Clint's laugh was dry, grating. "You honestly think I'm going to get in a car and ride away, leaving scum like you behind to 'protect' my fiancée? Who's going to protect her from you?"

Gary seemed on the verge of laughter. "Elise doesn't need protection from me. Her father trusts me."

"Well, I don't." Clint's neck suffused with red. "And I'm not leaving here without you."

Gary wasn't convinced. "Come on, Jessup. All

these months of exile and you expect me to believe you'd give up your little crusade because you don't want me to stay with Elise?"

"You'd better believe it," Clint bit out. He'd had to make a lot of concessions in the interest of cooperation, he thought. And nearly all of them had been painful. Not this time. This time they would cooperate with him. And at this late hour, they had no choice.

Sam came to the door, clad in a navy hooded jacket and holding another in his hand. "You ready, pal?"

Clint didn't budge. "I'm not leaving him here with her. If he stays, I stay."

"You could take me with you," Elise ventured again.

"I'm not taking you," Clint said, "and I'm not leaving him."

Sam looked at Gary, who had lost his smugness. "All right, Rivers. You're going with us. I'll get someone else to stay. Go get one of the jackets and put it on."

"But Cranston—"

"Cranston will understand," Sam said.

Shooting Clint one final, fiery glare, Gary left the room.

"What if he doesn't try to protect you?" Elise asked. "What if he—"

"He's a good cop, despite the fact that I detest him. He'll do his job," Clint assured her. "I'll be fine."

"He will," Sam said, tossing Clint the jacket he

held. "Put it on," he said. "With the hood up. It's the latest style in sniperproof wear."

"But you're wearing one too. What if they mistake you for me?"

"That's the general idea, pal. And if they see ten of us in the same jacket, we're liable to confuse the pants off of them."

"I'm looking forward to it," Clint said dryly.

Elise watched them both pull up the hood. "It's a good idea," she said in a shaky voice.

"It was your father's idea," Sam said. "Just like the ambulances."

"Ambulances?"

Sam nodded toward the front door. "Come on. You won't believe this."

Elise followed them out the door and caught her breath at the sight of ten officers wearing hooded navy jackets, milling around three ambulances.

"With everybody wearing the coats, and not a clue as to which ambulance holds the witness, there's not a whole lot they can do, is there?" Sam noted the apprehension still on Elise's face. "We'll bring him back this way too, Elise. We'll take care of him."

"Who's going to take care of you?" Karen asked from the side of the house, where she leaned pensively against the wall.

"I'll take care of myself, pretty lady," Sam said in a softer voice. The wind whipped Karen's hair across her mouth, and Sam stepped forward to push it back. "You'll be here when I get back?"

She shrugged and attempted a smile. "Where would I go?"

"Good point," he said. His hand lingered on her face, and his eyes softened. "I will be back, you know. I have this gut feeling."

"Hold onto it," she said, but her voice cracked.

The engines cranked to life, signifying that the time had come.

Elise clung tighter to Clint's arm, but she reached out for Sam's as well. "I haven't been very nice to you," she choked out, tears blurring her eyes. "But you've been good to Clint. Will you ride in the same car with him?"

A poignant smile sauntered across Sam's face. "You bet I will. And I expect to be best man in the wedding when we get back."

Elise nodded and lowered her eyes. She saw Gary look back at her with a sullen expression, and he got in one of the cars—thankfully not the one Clint was riding in. Clint took her face in gentle hands and kissed her one last time. "I love you, Elise," he whispered.

"I love you too, Superman," she said, before he turned and dashed into the ambulance.

She and Karen were left behind with three guards as the ambulances started their procession to Vicksburg and the trial.

"Are we all right?" Elise asked in a tremulous voice as the cars disappeared from sight.

"I hope so," was all Karen said before going into the house, to bask in her own despondency.

213

* * *

Karen was washing the dishes when Elise found her in the kitchen, stacking them on a drainer without anything under it to catch the water, but Elise didn't correct her. The fact that she was doing such a domestic chore at all was a major indication of her state of mind. She thought back, and realized that she had never seen Karen do it before.

A wet cup slipped from her hand and crashed onto the floor. Muttering a curse, Karen stooped to pick it up, but she turned her back to Elise when she saw her watching.

It was too late. Elise had already seen the rare tears forging shiny paths down her friend's face. Swallowing back her own fragile ball of emotion blocking her throat, Elise pulled out a chair and sat down. "I've been pretty caught up in my own troubles," she said. "I just realized that you're serious about Sam, aren't you?"

"Yeah." Karen gave a soft, unspirited laugh. "Imagine me falling for some guy who carries a gun and doesn't know where—or if—he's going to live from day to day."

"If anybody could, you could."

Karen wiped at her eyes and tossed the shattered remains of the cup into the trash can. "Are you implying that I fall too easily?"

"No. I wasn't even thinking of the Italian circus acrobat, or the paratrooper, or that guy who made like Evel Knievel every time he cranked up his bike." They both forced an attempt at a smile. "No, I meant that if anybody could handle some-

214

one with such an unpredictable occupation, you could. I've never met anybody with such acceptance. Such an ability to take one day at a time. I envy you for it. You put so much value on what you have, and don't even seem to worry about tomorrow."

New tears sprang into Karen's eyes to replace those she had wiped away, but she blinked them back. "Don't envy me, Elise. It's a defense mechanism. And it's slipping. Because I'm very worried right now." Her voice cracked with the admission.

Elise gazed solemnly at her for a moment. "Are you in love with him?"

Karen swallowed. "All I know is that when I'm with him, I'm shriveling up inside. His eyes make me warm. And when he kisses me . . ."

"He kisses you?" Somehow, Elise's image of Sam didn't fit that role.

Karen gave a soft smile. "When he kisses me, I burst all over. My hormones start screaming. And now that he's gone, I ache."

Elise didn't know what to say, for Karen had never been quite *that* serious.

"How long have I known the guy, anyway?"

"Three days?" Elise asked.

Karen shrugged. "It could have been three years."

"Maybe it'll be three more decades," Elise ventured.

"Or three more minutes," Karen whispered.

Elise's face contorted, and she covered her mouth to hold back the onslaught of despair.

"Don't, Karen. I need you to tell me that we'll be all right. That things will be great. I need you to offer me pistachios and a stack of work to get my mind off of it."

"I need the same things." The words were spoken on a gasp of restraint, but big tears spilled over her lashes and rolled down her cheeks.

Elise stood up and set her arm around her friend's shoulder. It was time to return the favor Karen had granted her for the past eight months. It was time to swallow back her own self-pity, to move past it, and to help her friend through this horror. "Could I interest you in some pistachios?" she asked.

Karen smiled through her tears. "I really should develop a taste for those." She wiped her eyes and pushed her blond hair back behind her ears.

"We could get drunk," Elise suggested.

Karen shook her head. "No booze. I've looked. You think I'd be in here washing dishes and blubbering if there was an alternative?"

"They'll be all right," Elise said, and she tried to believe it. And Karen tried too. "They're strong, and Sam is the best bodyguard Clint could hope for."

"But bodyguards have been known to stop bullets for the body they're guarding," Karen said. "And Sam feels a big responsibility to Clint."

"But they aren't the only two out there," she went on. "And they may be as close as you can come to being heroes, but they aren't stupid."

"No, they aren't stupid," Karen agreed. She

looked at the ceiling, as if tipping her head back could waylay the tears. "I should have brought my camera. I should have gotten a picture of him. I should have taped one of those ridiculous songs he kept singing. I should have . . ."

Elise pulled her against her shoulder and hushed her like a mother hushing a child. It had to be purged, this misery. This was Karen's purging time. She only hoped she could hold herself together long enough to see her dearest friend through it.

CHAPTER FOURTEEN

The sound of Sam's lamentably off-key singing tempered the low roar of the ambulance's engine, his slow voice coming across like a dirge rather than a pick-me-up as Clint was used to. He sat with his legs crossed on the stretcher, his head swaying slowly against the wall.

"How much farther?" Clint cut in uneasily. The technician's seat felt like a vibrating slab of concrete, and his heart raced in anticipation of something he couldn't even name.

The driver, adorned in a navy-blue bulletproof vest, glanced back over his shoulder. "About thirty more minutes. So far, so good."

So far, so good. Why did that sound like a countdown to doom? Clint wondered. And why the feeling eating at his gut that something terrible was going to happen—not to him, but to Elise?

"How well do you know those three cops we left back there?" he asked Sam.

Sam stopped humming. "Well enough to know I can trust them. You don't have to worry."

Another moment of silence followed, this time without Sam's singing. Clint watched him glance out the window, his eyes distant and full of thought. "She was really worried, you know," he said finally. He reached in his pocket and pulled out a pack of cigarettes. "She pretended not to be, but she was."

"Elise?"

"No, Karen. It's been a long time since anyone has worried about me."

A soft smile tugged at Clint's lips. "Becoming attached to the lady, are you?"

Instead of the usual quip, a pale shadow intruded on Sam's eyes, and he shrugged. "As much as a man like me can become attached."

"From knowing you the last eight months, pal, I'd say that's pretty attached."

Sam grinned. "What do you know?" His grin faded, and his gaze gravitated back toward the window. "I've gotten attached before. It nearly destroyed two pretty decent people."

"What? Your marriage?"

Sam swallowed and shook a cigarette out of the pack. "Yeah. I watched her turn from a level-headed, independent, cool woman into a basket case whenever I walked out the door. She was sure that one day I wouldn't come back." He sighed and shifted on the stretcher. "We both got bitter. I felt smothered and guilty and she got angrier and angrier. The best thing we ever did for each other was call it quits."

Clint watched Sam roll the cigarette filter

against his tongue, then light it, narrowing his eyes against the smoke wafting upward.

"Karen seems different, though." Sam's observation was set on the edge of hope, but couched in caution.

"Elise says she's had a tough life. Both parents died when she was pretty young. She takes things in stride, and doesn't dwell on things that would break most people."

"And she looks like a goddess," Sam tacked on. He reached to the oxygen cylinder and tapped it thoughtfully. "That silky hair, and those eyes . . ."

Clint couldn't suppress his laughter. "Man, you've got it bad."

Sam cocked a half-grin and leveled a look on his friend that held no denial. "Seen any of her pictures?"

Clint thought for a moment. He had been in her photography studio once. "Yeah. She's pretty good. It's all upbeat stuff. Ferris wheels, kids with candy all over their faces, bright-colored birds."

"No erotica?" Sam's grin was irrepressible.

"Depends on how you look at it, I guess." He thought about Karen, and how they had acted toward each other lately, as if they each disapproved of the other's way of caring for the common person they loved. Clint's eyes grew serious. "I get aggravated with her sometimes, but she's been good for Elise. Helped her through a hellish time. Elise has a short fuse, and she explodes emotionally just as quickly as she pulls in the reins. She can't stand to sit still and let things go by without her. That's why it was so hard on her when I left and there was absolutely nothing she could do about it. And Karen's get-on-with-life attitude was helpful to her."

"What do you think?" Sam's smile left his eyes, and a shadow of doubt crept into them. "You think a lady like that could be attracted to a deviate like me?"

Clint grinned. "What do *you* think? Has she run kicking and screaming away from you?"

Sam laughed. "Not since that first day." His laughter died in a sighing expiration, and he took the cigarette out of his mouth and contemplated it. "Matter of fact, she's gotten pretty close to me a time or two. Pretty darn close. I don't know, maybe there is hope."

"I wouldn't be surprised, buddy," Clint assured his friend. "There's always hope."

Hope became the thin thread that pulled Karen from the quicksand of her depression almost as quickly as she had plunged into it. After washing her face and brushing her hair, she came into the kitchen and informed Elise that it was time for them to look at the positive side.

"Is there one?" Elise cracked open another pistachio and dropped the shells on the pile growing on the table.

"Of course." Karen took a deep breath and began the recitation as if she'd rehearsed it. "The chances of anyone getting through that security barricade to either Clint or Sam are pretty slim.

And I trust your dad. He'll make sure that nothing happens to them on the way out, either."

"Give it up, Karen," Elise moaned. She popped a nut into her mouth. "I'm furious at my father, and I'm not interested in hearing how good and kind and conscientious he is. He had no right to do what he's done."

Karen sighed and sat on the table. "All right. We won't talk about it then. Let's just go watch television."

"Television? There's nothing on television in the middle of the day."

Karen cast her a disbelieving look. "Surely, you can't be serious. I realize that you spend most of your waking moments revamping nature's mistakes with water, but you can't have completely missed the soap operas in all these years."

"I hate to break this to you, but . . ."

"Then don't. Some of the greatest stories ever woven are on the soaps. On this one I watch, there's a girl who's a KGB agent, but she has amnesia and thinks she's a hairdresser. Only Russia has a little disk in her tooth, and they record everything she says or does with her CIA husband. Come on, it's great. I'll narrate for you. It'll get your mind off your problems. *No one* can have problems worse than those people." Karen grabbed the bag of pistachios and hopped off of the table, starting toward the living room.

Resigned to letting Karen's methods of diverting her fears and anxiety help her, and desperate for those pistachios, Elise followed her friend out of the kitchen.

Eric Cranston paced in his own kitchen in Vicksburg thirty minutes later, his hand trembling as he held the telephone. "I don't care what she said!" he shouted to one of the police officers guarding Elise. "Get my daughter on the telephone immediately or I'll have your badge!"

"I'm sorry, sir. She refuses to talk to you. I tried to—"

"Don't give me *tried!* Tell her I *order* her to get on this phone!"

The young officer muffled the phone with his hand while he relayed the message. Cranston dumped his uneaten breakfast into the garbage disposal and searched the cabinet for an antacid to stop the burning in his stomach. If he could just hear her voice, he thought, he could be assured that she was completely safe. The timing was crucial here, and after a sleepless night going over every angle to assure Clint's safety en route to court, it had finally occurred to him that it wasn't Clint's life that would be in jeopardy today. He was too well guarded, and Givanti's cohorts wouldn't risk the publicity of Clint's death. But what if they managed to get to Elise? What if his daughter were used as the go-between to keep Clint from testifying honestly?

After a moment, the young officer cleared his throat. "Uh . . . sir. I gave her the order, and she said she didn't care."

"DIDN'T CARE?" Cranston bellowed.

The phone was snatched from the officer's hand, and Cranston heard his daughter say, "Give me that!"

Cranston's blood pressure dropped a degree, along with his voice. "Elise?"

"I have nothing to say to you, Dad, so you're wasting your valuable time trying to call me."

"I just wanted to see if you're all right. I've been very worried about you."

"It's Clint you should be worried about," she said. "He's the one you've made into your pawn." Her voice cracked and faltered, and she swallowed. "Has he made it there yet?"

"Not yet," her father said. "But I don't expect them for twenty minutes or so." He cleared his throat and looked down at the oak grain on his kitchen table. "It's going to be all right, sweetheart, but I want you to be careful."

Tears sprang to Elise's eyes. Tears of anger, tears of fear, tears of betrayal. "If anything happens to him, Dad, I'll never forgive you." She caught her breath on a sob and pressed a fist into her eyes. "I'll probably never forgive you, anyway."

Cranston slumped down in his chair and tried to picture the little pigtailed girl with the sapphire eyes who had been his very life. "When it's over, I'll come there and we'll talk . . ."

"There's nothing I have to say to you," she snapped. "You've used the man I love like a toy to satisfy your legal ego, and you've lied to me to do it. Go back to work, Dad. Go make Clint spill his guts. Then bask in the glory of the press and your awed followers. I won't be there."

The phone slammed in Cranston's ear like a clap of thunder that reached straight through to his soul, shaking him free of everything in his life that had meaning.

The telephone was cold beneath Elise's trembling hand, as cold as the betrayal she felt. Karen's soap opera wasn't going to do the trick, she thought miserably, and neither were the pistachios. She needed to think. She needed to be alone.

Pinching the bridge of her nose, she turned back to the officer who had answered the phone. "I want to go out to the pier and catch my breath."

The young man still looked shaken by his run-in with the district attorney, but he ran a hand through his recently cut hair and got his sunglasses. "I'll come with you."

She squelched the urge to scream about her need to be alone. The poor guy looked as if he'd had enough. "If you have to," she said. "But I need to be alone."

"You won't even know I'm there," he said. "Not unless you need me."

Quickly, before Karen could insist on joining her, too, she darted out the door and made her way to the pier. Treading out to the end of it, she sat down and crossed her feet. Hugging her knees to her chest, she looked out over the water. The sun hadn't climbed very high in the sky, but already the air was sweltering. From somewhere upwind on the still reservoir, she heard children laughing and the sound of a ski boat farther down. She wondered what it would be like to have nothing to worry about again. Here, in this isolated section on the still water, she could almost pretend she was a lazy socialite out for a tan. So peaceful, she thought. So private. One would never know that the end of her world could be lurking just around the corner.

Would they contact her if Clint was hurt en route to court? Or would her father insist on "protecting" her again? A fresh surge of anger shot through her, and a renegade tear paved its way down her face. What would she do if Clint didn't come back to her?

What was she doing? She caught herself and shook her head, as if the violent movement would shake her back to her senses. How could she think about what she would do if he didn't come back? She hadn't given up already. Even when he had disappeared for eight months, she had never given up entirely.

She dropped her head onto her knees, and reached deeply inside herself for the strength to endure what she was facing. If only it would rain. Rain cleansed and soothed and purged. It had always been a great source of comfort to her. She looked up into the sky and issued a silent prayer for strength. The prayer brought back a memory . . . a night months after her mother had died, when she'd felt her father's misery and his over-wrought worry for her, and the only escape she had found was on the sun roof jutting out from her bedroom window. It had been raining, and she remembered the whip of lightning in the distance, the chortle of thunder, and the cold, cruel prickles of hard rain upon her skin. But she had not been afraid. The storm had drowned out the pain and memories inside the house, and she had seen the lightning as flashes of future trying to break into her world and promise her something better. Something as comforting as the past.

She remembered how long she had sat out there, how cold she had become, yet the thought of going back in and facing her mourning father, buried in his work, had been too overwhelming. She remembered his fear when he'd found her out there after searching for over an hour, and her guilt for making him worry even more.

He had read her the riot act about being so foolish, then changed her clothes and dried her hair and tucked her into bed, struggling to keep back his own tears and concentrating on parental sternness instead. And even while he had lectured to her about lightning and pneumonia and falling off the slippery roof, she had known he loved her.

Perhaps too much. And that love had lead him into lying about the fate of another person she had allowed herself to love.

If only there were a roof she could climb on today, she thought, and distant lightning glittering on the slanting rain. If only there were some escape from this hell she and Clint were being dragged through. If only she had some guarantees . . .

* * *

Clint closed his eyes and tried to stay calm. They'd be there soon, and there had been no attempts made to stop them. In moments he would be inside the courtroom, waiting to tell everything he'd seen on that night eight months ago. He hoped it was worth it. He hoped Givanti would be locked up for the rest of his life.

He opened his eyes again and saw Sam sitting erect and alert, peering between the front seats out the windshield for some sign of danger. Maybe there wouldn't be any. Maybe Givanti's arms didn't reach far enough to . . .

"Holy hell!" The driver slammed on his brakes and screeched into a slanted halt, barely missing the ambulance in front of them. "What the—?"

"It's a tree." Sam's face turned white at the sight of the fallen tree obstructing their passage. He pulled his gun and held it toward the ceiling. "Someone doesn't want us to get through."

"Well, what do they think we'll do?" The driver's voice was strained, tremulous. "Just give up? It may delay things a little bit, but obviously it won't stop us completely."

Sam's eyes were straining up toward the small clay cliffs overlooking I-20. Clint's stomach plummeted. It wasn't the tree that was the problem. It was the fact that they were forced into being still.

The door to the ambulance in front of them opened, and two officers, one Clint recognized as Gary Rivers with his hood pulled down, got out and ran toward the tree. "Damn," Sam muttered.

228

"If anyone's watching, their getting out will tell them that obviously that's not the car you're in. By the process of elimination, they'll know you're either in the first one or this one. Damn! Turn around. Now! We've got to get out of here."

Helplessness and despair washed over Clint as he watched the two men run toward the tree and try to drag it out of the road. And then they began to back their ambulance up, when the ground erupted in an explosion that left the world before them in flames and debris and a whirl of smoke from which there seemed no escape.

"Elise!" Karen's voice was racked with horror as she screamed her name from the doorway of the house. "Oh, God! Elise come here!"

A moment of panic froze her, but then she pulled herself together and got up to run toward her friend, the officer guarding her close on her heels. "What happened? Did some—?"

"I don't know." Karen's voice trembled. "I was watching television, and the program was interrupted by a special bulletin. There was an explosion on I-20. An ambulance. One man was killed, three wounded."

"What?" Blood drained from her heart, leaving her dizzy. "No. It wasn't them. It was—"

The television sliced across her words as another bulletin came to life, this time from the steps of the courthouse, ". . . where we've been told the mystery witness in the Givanti trial was supposed to make his appearance half an hour ago. However, it is rumored that the witness is being transported in an ambulance, which may very well be the one that was in the explosion on I-20. We have no further information at this time, but we will be waiting here for word and will keep you informed. Please stay tuned for further updates."

One of the officers guarding them rushed for the telephone and began dialing frantically, and Elise and Karen crouched together and stared at the television. He was dead, Elise thought. It had happened, just as she knew it would . . .

The woman on the steps of the courthouse flashed back onto the screen, microphone in hand, her words tumbling out in a burst of excitement.

". . . ambulance has just arrived . . . witness is unharmed and on his way in . . ."

Elise clutched her face and gave in to the tears racking her. "Oh, thank God. He's not dead!"

The camera switched to the group of navy-blue hooded men, with guns pulled, huddled together around the "witness," rushing for the door. "We understand that the explosion was believed to be an attempt to stop the witness from testifying, and that the attack is not allowed as evidence in the trial. So the jury will not have the benefit of this information that seems to implicate the defendant." She paused and listened as someone relayed a piece of information to her. "We understand that the men in the burning car were police officers trying to divert the potential attacks, and they succeeded at their own expense. We're told the explosion was caused by a grenade thrown from the cliff over the highway, and that the assailant remains at large."

"It wasn't Sam," Karen choked out. "They were in the other car. Thank God, it wasn't them."

Not yet, a voice inside Elise despaired. Clint and Sam had made it to court. But would they make it back? How many chances would they have for escape before the lunatics stalking them succeeded?

Numbly, she got up and went upstairs to the room she and Clint had shared the night before. It still smelled of shower steam and after-shave, but it seemed so cold here without him. So dark. Turning on the light, she pivoted slowly, taking inventory of the things he had left. The shirt he had worn yesterday draped over the chair; the worn pair of jeans crumpled on the floor; his old jogging shoes. She picked up the shirt and shrugged into it, burying her face in the lapels. Taking a deep, fortifying breath, she inhaled its scent. It smelled like Clint: strong and masculine.

Biting her lip, as though it would keep her from falling apart, she reached for the box of letters he had written to her, and she thought how she should have told him of the ones she had written. She crawled onto the bed and opened it, needing those letters to get her through the day. They were all she had of him until he came back.

And they all began with "My Elise." She lifted the top one and tried to read the shaky scrawl.

They tell me the infection's gone, and the scar

should heal over soon. But there's nothing they can do for the feeling of emptiness inside me. There's no medication that can heal my spirit. Because I know you're hurting, just as badly as I did when Jake rammed that knife into my side. At least I understood what I was going through. You have no idea.

If you could wait until I've served my sentence in hell, I'll come back to you someday. And if there's such a thing as justice, and if God is kind, we'll start our lives over again.

I love you. I wish I could convince your father to deliver this to you, but he won't. I suppose he knows best in these matters, but I hate letting you think that a love like mine could die. Even if I do, my love never will.

Elise closed her eyes and a tear dropped onto the ink, smearing it. He had believed he would die. He hadn't expected to survive those months. And all the while she was sitting at home feeling sorry for herself for having to return the wedding gifts and cancel the wedding plans. She had thought it was the end of the world. But Clint had known it firsthand.

She picked up another letter, and saw that the handwriting was much clearer.

What would I do without Sam? He listens when I talk about you, and he never acts bored or unsympathetic. I think he probably knows everything about you there is to know, right down to the time you spilt pink lemonade on your head. We got a good laugh out of that one. It was good, because there's so little to laugh about these days.

I hope it's not the same with you. I hope you can still laugh, and enjoy, and love life. I hope your eyes still light up when you go outside in the mornings and see that it's going to be a beautiful day. I hope you still feel that sense of purpose that has always been so unique about you. If I've gotten anything from all of this, it is a more defined sense of purpose. I'm doing the right thing, and if that's the only consolation I ever get from it, it'll have to be enough.

I've taken up jogging and working out to lift my spirits. It gives me a boost. Sam sings. It makes him feel better, and though I'll never admit it to him, it makes me feel better too. As long as there's a song for him to sing and a path for me to jog, and your face in my dreams, I'll get through this. And you will too.

She couldn't help smiling at the uplifting tone of that one. She wiped the tears off her face and went on to the next one.

It's so lonely without you. So quiet. So cold. There are days when I think that just seeing your face would get me through another few months. The thought itself gets me through another day. If only there were some end in sight.

I'll never be comfortable in our love again. When I get back to you, I'm going to see every day with you as the dawning of another chance to affirm what I feel for you. I love you in a dimension removed from all this madness. You're the tenderest, gentlest part of me. You're the very life that keeps me breathing.

Are you still wearing your hair the same? Does

233

your bottom lip still feel like warm, wet satin? Are your eyes still putting the sky to shame? Oh, God, how I want to hold you. Please, just hold on a little longer. Just a little longer.

"Just a little longer," Elise whispered, nodding her head. "I'll hold on, Clint. I'll hold on."

CHAPTER FIFTEEN

"Did you take the pulse of the man you said was shot?" The defense attorney's acrimonious voice was directed to Clint, though he faced the jury. After hours of drilling testimony, in which Southern analyzed everything he dared to say, Clint was getting angry.

"No, I did not."

"Then how can you know that he was dead?"

"He had a bullet hole in his chest. And I heard Jake *say* he was dead."

"Did you examine the alleged bullet wound?"

Clint smirked and shook his head with disbelief. "No, I did not. Under the circumstances I thought it a little silly to pop out from where I was hiding and ask them to let me examine the body so that my testimony in the murder trial might be flawless."

A soft roar of chuckles passed over the spectators, then died.

"Did you see them bury the body?"

"No, I did not."

"Did you see them throw it into the river?"

"No."

"Did you attend the funeral of this man you say was dead?"

"Of course not."

"Could that be because there wasn't a funeral?"

"I don't know if there was. I was busy recovering from my knife wound at the time and didn't much care."

Southern's back went rigid and he swung around to the judge. "Your honor, I want that last comment stricken from the record. It has no relevance in this case."

The judge nodded gruffly. "Sustained."

The defense attorney's eyes were beaded shards of coal, leveled on Clint's as he faced him squarely, preparing for a duel. "In other words, Mr. Jessup, this man that you are saying was killed on the night in question could in fact be walking around right now. You really have no evidence at all that he was even harmed."

"Do you consider blood evidence?" Clint's question came through steely lips.

"People bleed, Mr. Jessup. They also heal."

Clint would be damned if he'd spent the last eight months in hell just to have some hyped-up lawyer shoot his story down. He'd seen what he'd seen. "I saw Givanti shoot him!" he blared. "I saw him fall, and I saw blood on the left side of his chest! I heard—"

"But did you touch him? Did you know for sure—"

"I heard Givanti and Jake say that he was dead, and I—"

"But did *you* know beyond a shadow of a doubt—"

"And I heard them decide to hide the body and then drag him out!"

The attorney's face was raging red, and the exchange was at top volume and rising in pitch.

"For all you know, Mr. Jessup, he could have gotten up and walked home after that! The body was never found!"

"Then why have so many attempts been made on my life? Why was I stabbed and practically blown up? Why was Gary Rivers killed just hours ago?"

"Your honor, this testimony is—"

Clint bolted up. "Why were threats made on my fiancée's life? Why was it so important that they keep me from talking?"

". . . irrelevant! This must be stricken from the record!"

"Why hasn't this Anderson man come forward if he's still alive? I can't show you a dead body to back up my story, but you can't show me a live one to back up yours! Can you?"

"Your honor, I'd like to request a short recess." It was the prosecuting attorney's voice which cut across that of the two battling men's this time.

Clint dropped back into his chair on the witness stand and held his face in his hands. He'd be damned if that man was going to get away with this! He would absolutely be damned!

* * *

Clint tapped his fingers on the arm of the chair he sat in, and wished to heaven that he smoked. At least then he'd have something to do with his hands. When Cranston and Breard had stepped in quietly just moments ago, he had not been sure whether it was anger or delight sparkling in their eyes. He didn't much care.

"I could lecture you on the importance of keeping your cool in the courtroom, Clint," Breard said, "but under the circumstances, I think your outburst has been to our advantage. Especially the part about your recovering from your knife wound."

It wasn't the event that was significant, Clint thought, but the telling of it.

"He struck it from the record. It doesn't matter that people have been hurt over this. My knife wound is as insignificant to those people as Gary Rivers's death was."

"Oh, it matters, all right. The jury heard every word, whether it's on the transcript or not."

"But what difference will it make when he comes back in there and makes them believe that Anderson is alive and well and living in Kalamazoo somewhere? I *wish* he hadn't been killed that night!" You have no idea how many times I've wished that. If he hadn't been shot, Rivers and Jake and his brother would be alive, and I wouldn't have even had to testify. You've got the drug charges wrapped up without me. But I never counted on having to prove that the guy I

238

saw shot in the chest was really dead when they dragged him out!"

Cranston was calm. "You did a good job this morning telling play-by-play what happened. The jury hasn't forgotten. And honestly, I think what just happened in the courtroom did more to make Southern look bad than you." He poured water from a sweating silver pitcher into a glass and drank from it. "He lost the reins when you stood up and started yelling, and he couldn't get them back. His loss of his cool showed a little trace of desperation. I expect him to try to get some witnesses in here to smear your character. His last resort is to convince the jury that your word isn't worth anything."

"Smear my character? How?"

"He'll find a way."

"I don't know how," Clint mumbled. "My life is clean. My crimes seem to be only in the mind. Unless I'm wrong, there's no crime against wanting to strangle someone."

"Let's hope you're right," Cranston said, patting Clint's knee with fatherly fondness. "But we'll be prepared just in case."

Clint sat in knots for the rest of the day as he heard friends and acquaintances testifying to his character. It was brought out that he was undependable. Hadn't he quit his job in the middle of a crucial project? Hadn't he done that twice?

Cranston's face blazed fire when the defense attorney filtered from someone that Clint was engaged to the daughter of the district attorney. In

239

spite of Breard's string of objections, the job had been done, and Clint looked like a man whose very words inspired doubt an ally of a prosecutor out to get the defendant.

Although Breard had the opportunity for rebuttal, Clint had a deep, sinking feeling that it was all for naught. And the hopelessness and frustration and tension rising inside him became a volatile mixture while he listened to the closing statements in the trial, and watched the jury being dismissed to decide on the verdict.

"The jury could be out for days," Clint told Cranston in a voice that denoted the calm before the storm. "I'm not going to be kept here. I want to get back to Elise. She must be out of her mind worrying." He paced back and forth before the black tinted window and tried to dispel the feeling that he was smothering. He needed air, and quiet, and an hour in which this damnable trial didn't hang foremost in his mind. Sam's cigarette smoke floated upward on the stale air, and his quiet scrutiny told Clint that he, too, dreaded the verdict.

"Don't you care about the outcome of the trial?" Cranston asked. He sat at his desk, going back over his notes, trying to second-guess the twelve men and women who held this situation in their hands. But Clint had the suspicious feeling that that wasn't Cranston's real concern.

"Of course I do. But it won't surprise me if Givanti gets off. The last eight months of my life have been like something out of the theater of the

240

absurd, anyway. A big farce. Might as well end it accordingly."

"I disagree. I think the jury will bring in a guilty verdict. Meanwhile, I'd like to keep you here."

Clint stopped and pointed a warning finger at Cranston. "You can't make me stay," Clint warned. "I'm going back to Elise."

Cranston's face reddened, and he thumped his forehead with an index finger and compressed his lips.

"Look, I did what I was supposed to do. I don't regret it, no matter what comes of it. But I'm not going to put my life on hold any longer."

Cranston got up, shrugged out of his coat, and hung it over his chair. A slash of perspiration beaded over his lip. "I'm just asking you to wait a little longer. Until we can be sure that things have settled down."

"Settled down?" Clint's laugh bordered on hysteria. "Are you kidding me? You think things will settle down just like that? You think I don't know that Givanti will get revenge? That's why I want to get back to Elise!"

"That's why I want you here!" Cranston bellowed, slamming his hand on his desk. "I'm trying to protect my daughter! I'm trying to protect *you,* damn it! Don't be blind, man!"

"I'm not blind! But I want to protect Elise too. She's probably sitting there thinking the danger's here. But if *I* were Givanti and wanted to get revenge, I wouldn't send my goons to the courthouse to make an example of the witness. I'd teach him a lesson by taking it out on the person who means the most to him. I'd—"

"Exactly what I'm getting at!" Cranston cried. "And the closer you are to her—"

"The more protection I can give her. I have to be there to make sure that she's safe and doesn't get careless. *You* can't be there, and those guards barely even know her."

Sam, who had sat quietly in the corner rubbing his jaw, stood up. "Let him go back," he said. "I won't let anything happen to them. I haven't so far, have I?"

"By the grace of God, no," Cranston admitted. "But I don't like it."

"There *is* no safe place," Sam pointed out dolefully. "Not really. Beef up security some more. Pack our cars full this time. All we really have to do is wait to see if we're right about Givanti's little ring being small. Frankly, I think it is. But while we're waiting for the verdict, there's no use making everyone suffer more."

"But some lunatic is still out there. The one who tried to blow you up on the way here." Cranston's voice broke. "What if—?"

"I can protect them." Sam's voice was unwavering.

"All right," the man said, sinking down into a chair and looking suddenly much older than his years. "All right. Go ahead. I'll be there as soon as the verdict comes in. For God's sake, man, be careful."

"I'll die before I'll let anything happen to Elise," Clint said.

Cranston looked up at him and managed a smile. "Well, how about if we keep both of you alive? I'd sort of like to have grandchildren."

"You'll get them," Clint promised him, his own dark eyes sparkling at the prospect. "You have my word on that one."

The President of the United States could not have boasted more security than Clint had as they left the courthouse that evening. Again donning their hooded jackets, this time they had some twenty police officers accompanying them in the three ambulances, one of which had been replaced since the mishap earlier that day. On a dark, empty side road they changed from the ambulances into the trailer of an eighteen-wheeler and finished the journey, catching up to a convoy of unsuspecting truckers with which they blended nicely.

Sam had brought along a transistor radio, and when a news bulletin interrupted to say that the jury had just delivered the verdict on the Givanti trial, he quieted everyone.

Twenty men held their breath collectively as the man's voice said, "Givanti was found guilty on both charges . . ."

A loud cheer of approval sounded throughout the dark trailer, with each man patting another on the back, but Clint was quiet. Givanti had been found guilty because of his testimony, but somehow he didn't feel that the nightmare was over. Somehow it just seemed to be entering a new phase.

* * *

Elise stepped out of the bath and pulled Clint's robe around her. He was on his way back to her, and she wasn't going to think about the fact that he might not make it.

Quietly, she padded into the bedroom, and unwrapped the candles she had found in the cabinet downstairs. With trembling hands, she set them up around the room. She wouldn't think about fear or death tonight, she thought. She wouldn't think about the possibility that Givanti would go free. And she wouldn't think about Gary Rivers.

Gary, who had been hurt when she fell in love with Clint. Gary, who had only wanted to protect her. Gary, who had died protecting Clint.

It was meant to be, she told herself, lifting her chin. The price for life was high, and this time fate had expended one life for another.

She wouldn't feel guilty that she hadn't argued for Gary when he'd wanted to stay with her. She wouldn't feel guilty that she had wanted him to go. And—God help her—she wouldn't feel guilty for being safe and alive when so many others had suffered.

She would simply prepare this room to be a haven for the man she loved. He would need it when he came back to her. He would need peace. He would need love. And he would need for her to understand the sorrow and grief and self-incrimination etched on his heart for the rest of his life.

Just as it was etched on hers.

"Here they come!" Karen darted out the door as the headlights of the huge truck bumped down the road toward the house.

Elise followed her into the night, her heart fluttering. She wouldn't relax, wouldn't be able to allay this cold sweat she was in, wouldn't be able to stop trembling, until she was in Clint's arms again and could *feel* that he was safe.

The door to the trailer was opened, and a loud, cocky voice wafted across the breeze singing "Duke of Earl" off-key. "Duke-duke-duke, duke of Earl, duke-duke, duke of Earl . . ." Sam appeared at the doorway to the trailer, dancing like a fifties' teen idol with an imaginary microphone.

When he saw Karen, he sped up the tempo and hopped down, and took her in his arms to pirouette her and then do a mock, rock 'n' roll waltz across the yard. "Duke-duke, duke of Earl . . ."

Karen's giggle rang across the night, lending a note of unreality to the tragedies that had transpired today. It was as if she believed it was all over . . .

Clint came to the door and jumped out, his eyes immediately connecting with hers. Elise felt the love and relief in his look, and suddenly the events of the day fled her mind as well. He was here. He had come back. And no one could take him away from her again.

Through the men milling around them, he came to her, and she buried herself in his arms.

"I was so afraid," she choked.

"I was so worried," he breathed.

"You're all right," they said together.

His kiss was ambrosia, warm molten joy, a fragment of heaven. In it she found security and life, future and past, her heart and her soul. The taste of salt tears brought his head back, and he kissed them away, clutching her like a treasure that he would guard with his life.

"Have you eaten?" she whispered irrelevantly.

"Not hungry," he breathed against her ear, sending shivers to scamper down her neck. "I just want you. I just need you."

"Oh, Clint," she whispered. "Don't ever leave me again. Don't ever let me go. Promise me."

"I promise, baby," he said. "I promise." His eyes narrowed painfully, and he pulled back to look at her. "Elise, Gary's dead. He—"

Elise's eyes welled into glittering blue half-moons, and she set her fingers over his lips. "Don't . . . don't say it. I already know." She caught her breath on a soft sob. "Please. Let it just be us. Let's not talk about . . ." Her voice trailed off, and she couldn't go on.

Clint scooped her up in his arms and pushed through the men and into the house, oblivious to the crowd and the questions and the cheering. She laid her face against his neck and wept quietly, so grateful for his warmth, his compassion, his strength. Thankfully, no one stopped him as he took her up to his room.

It smelled of candles and had a yellow cast to it from the tiny flames flickering in the darkness. She lifted her head to gauge his reaction. "I wanted it to be peaceful for you," she whispered.

246

"I wanted it to be like a little square of paradise, where we could pretend that we were normal and happy and innocent."

Clint swallowed and pressed his forehead against hers. *Innocent.* Did she feel as guilty as he? Had her innocence been lost in this madness? A new surge of despair washed over him, but when she kissed the indentation in his neck and brushed her hands through his hair, he forgot it.

He swallowed and sought out the source of the slow, seductive violin concerto that filled the room.

"I found a tape player downstairs," she whispered. "They had Bach."

"Bach." The word was murmured in a cracked voice, and his black eyes shone with a luster that would forever brighten her heart. He set her on the bed and sat down next to her. "And a couple of hours ago I thought it would take months for me to feel peace again."

"For now," she whispered. "We have it for now." In her timorous voice was an unspoken plea not to think about the demons of fear and hazard that lurked only a heartbeat away.

He leaned over to nibble her neck, and she shivered. "They dragged you into the trial. They said I'd had an affair with a co-op student."

The past, she thought. The past was better . . . before they knew of the fragility of life and love, before they had known how easily it could slip away from them.

She arched her neck and closed her eyes. "You did have an affair with a co-op student."

"Not until you had graduated." He unbuttoned the top button of her blouse and bared a bit of her shoulder for his lips.

"But we fell in love long before that. And in our minds, we made love every time we looked at each other."

His hand moved up her side, to her breast, but his lips made a slow journey down her shoulder. "Do you know what those eyes did to me back then? Whenever I looked at you, I felt dizzy. Did you know that?"

She released one more button for him, and he pulled her shirt further down her arm. "No. I was too mesmerized myself. I kept waiting for you to make a move, and you never did. The night I graduated I thought I'd take a gamble and see how far I could push you. But I didn't have to push at all."

"All I wanted was to make love to you." His breath whispered across her chest, and her breast strained against his hand. "And I had to sit through all the toasts, and suffer through all the congratulations, and all I could think about was how I'd get you out of there."

With trembling hands, she freed the rest of the buttons on her blouse, and he opened it. A long sigh escaped him at her bared breasts, and he cupped them and lowered his face to them. "You were so easy to love," he whispered. "And you loved so thoroughly." He took a nipple in his mouth and circled it with his tongue. She felt it clear to her core, and gasped at the release. "You trembled then too."

248

"You've always made me tremble," she murmured.

"You tasted like champagne and perfume and desire. And you made my heart ache." He slipped her blouse completely off and unbuttoned his shirt. Her hands against his bare skin made his pulse sprint as she slid it off his arms.

"And you tasted like beer and wind and passion," she said. "And you made my soul cry."

"Did I?"

She trailed her fingers through his hair, and crushed her breasts against his chest. "Yes. Because I loved you. And you loved me."

His lips found hers again, and his tongue marked its claim, painting her soul in colors that would make it smile. Two hearts came together; two pairs of hands savored and touched.

His callused hand slipped down her bare, silky back and into the denim covering her. "Your clothes just seemed to slip off that night," he murmured breathlessly against her lips. With his free hand, he unclasped the front of her jeans and pulled the zipper down. His body quaked against her. "And now they seem like the Berlin Wall."

"Yours too." Her voice was husky. She unzipped his pants, then worked them down over his hips. "I don't remember how I got them off of you that night. I just remember how perfectly our bodies fit together, and how complete I was when you were inside me."

When they were both free of their clothes, she lowered him down on the bed. His hands moved across her body as she moved above him in slow, tantalizing seduction, making him close his eyes straining not to roll her beneath him and take her with all the passion swelling within him.

"I . . . can't . . . stand it," he groaned as she gave him pleasure that made every dimension of his being ache, every part of his body tremble.

When she herself could take no more, she moved him inside her, gasping at the depth and fulfillment. He rocked into her, guiding her hips with his hands until she was in a realm where ecstasy conquers. She came down slowly, but he was there to bring her back. He rolled her over on her side, and kept up the rhythm as she gasped and moaned and murmured against his neck. Then clinging to him, she felt herself hurl yet again into the outer reaches of fantasy, bursting lights playing kaleidoscopic games in her head. And when she returned, he rolled her onto her back.

"From now on when I make love to you," he whispered on a sparse husk of breath, "I'll remember tonight, and our little square of paradise."

As he spoke he slowed his rhythm, moving farther and harder, until she dug her fingernails into his skin. He closed his mouth over hers to muffle her cries, his tongue moving in the same fashion as his body. And once again, she felt a bursting from her very core, filling her with a heat that made her shimmer and glow.

And then he erupted inside her with throbbing force, his body quaking over hers, their breath mingling, their love filling every corner of their hearts. Enough to last past the present, past the paradise that was a moment of escape, past the fantasy that kept them sane . . . Even if it was destined to be snatched from them.

CHAPTER SIXTEEN

The smell of impending rain feathered up on the breeze, and the water seemed restless. The activity inside had settled as each man found a way to make himself useful, and Karen suddenly found herself outside alone with Sam—that is, as alone as was possible with twenty guards alert for battle.

Sam had danced her to the bank of the reservoir, the inky water reflecting the clouds in the sky and the partial moon that cast an eerie glow.

"So when do you get to go home?" she asked tentatively, quietly.

"Soon, I hope. I'll have to go into my apartment with a sandblaster to get rid of the cobwebs."

"Is it in Vicksburg?"

"Where else?"

"I could help. I'm great with cobwebs. I did a photographic layout of some once for a scientific magazine."

"I'd like to see it," Sam said. He pulled out a cigarette and his lighter, and cupped his hand against the wind to light it. "Do you do self-portraits?"

Karen grinned self-consciously and gathered her hair back to keep it from slapping into her face. "A self-portrait seems a little pointless."

"That all depends on whose self it is," he said, matching her grin. "I wouldn't mind having a pretty face framed on my wall to wake up to every morning."

She couldn't believe she was blushing. "Well, when I get home I'll look through my portfolio for one. I've done some gorgeous models . . ."

He touched her nose, let his finger glide over its tip and settle on her lips. "I said self-portraits. I want the photographer's face on my wall."

Letting her smile fade and her eyes widen, Karen straightened his collar and looked up into his sterling eyes. "I'll tell you what. I'll make you a self-portrait, if you'll give me a recording of 'Betty Lou's Gettin' Out Tonight.' "

Sam's fatuous grin was all over his face. "Sure. I can tape Bob Seger in a minute."

"Not Bob Seger," she said, her voice lowering to a seductive pitch. "I want to wake up to *your* voice every morning."

His smile faded, and his eyes sparkled like polished chrome. "That could be arranged," he whispered. "And you wouldn't even need a tape."

"No tape, no picture," she challenged softly.

"There must be some other alternative," he said, his lips slowly descending to hers.

"Maybe we can come up with something."

And as he kissed her, Karen vowed that this attachment would not end in misery.

Elise heard the sound of a car coming up the road, and as if the doom she dreaded had at last arrived, she pulled off of the bed and peered through the curtains. Some of the guards met the car, and even in the darkness she saw her father's large form unfolding from the car. "My dad," she told Clint, who lay staring at the ceiling as if, too soon, their moment of blissful peace had been shattered.

"Go easy on him, Elise," he whispered. "He's a good man with a tough job. And he loves you."

Elise leaned back against the wall, dejection in every line of her body as she pulled on her jeans and shrugged on her blouse. "Yeah, well I have a few things to say to him about the way he loves," she said with soft scorn. "He had no right to manipulate our lives the way he did."

"He also had no choice." Clint sat up and reached for the pair of jeans draped over the chair where he'd left them yesterday. "It would have happened whether he had been in charge or not."

She buttoned her blouse and watched as he dressed. "There were better ways, Clint." The judgment was uttered on a weary sigh.

Clint strode toward her and threaded his fingers through the rich, tousled roots at her nape. "And what were they? I've asked myself a million times, weren't there better ways. I've never been able to come up with any."

Elise looked out the window again, and Clint's hand slid to her shoulder. Her father was coming toward the house with the imperial posture of a king returning victoriously from war. She could refuse to talk to him, but she had too much to say. Too much rage to vent, for the war had cost too much. "Well, I have," she said, and started for the door.

Clint followed her.

Eric Cranston's seasoned, handsome face lit up at the sight of his daughter bouncing down the stairs. The light died, however, when she stood before him, bitterness and rage battling for a forum in her eyes.

"Hi, honey."

Elise propped her elbow on the banister and sent her father a dull, impassive gaze. "You got what you wanted, Dad. I don't think we have anything more to say to each other."

Cranston sighed heavily and reached for her. "Honey, I know you're upset. It's been trying for all of us."

"Has it?" Elise stepped away from her father's touch. Vicious heat started at her neck and rose to color the rise of her cheekbones. "Did you get stabbed? Did anyone try to blow you up? Did you have to give up eight months of your life for a cause?"

"Elise, you have to under—"

"Did anyone lie to you, and tell you that the person you love most in the world just decided he didn't want you anymore and took off for new horizons?"

255

"I did what I thought was best. I followed my judgment."

"Well, your judgment stinks!" Her voice hurled hoarsely across the room, knocking the wind from the older man.

"Don't you think I paid?"

"No. I think you gained a lot more than we lost. I think you're the hero now. You got your conviction. So what if people had to die for it?"

"A lot more people might have died if I hadn't! Including my daughter!"

She came toward him, her eyes like daggers. "Your daughter *did* die! When she thought the man she was going to marry had abandoned her. When she thought he was a criminal to run from. When she found out that his life might not last another day. I'm *still* dying, Dad! Because I know that whoever tried to blow Clint up in that ambulance today is probably not going to give up until he succeeds. Was your conviction worth it, Dad? Was it?"

"Elise, stop it!" Clint's order rang out, slicing through her anger. He looked at her with the intimacy of a lover, but with the sternness of a man who saw clearly on a day when the world was in a blur. "No one forced me to be a witness. If you have to lash out at someone, lash out at me for seeing what I saw. Lash out at Jake for making a mess of all our lives. Lash out at Givanti for killing Anderson. But don't lash out at your father for being put in the position where he had to do his job. If he'd handled it any other way, one or both of us might be dead right now. You know it and I know it!"

Elise clutched her head. "It's such a mess!" Her voice broke, and she started for the door. "I just want to get away from it. I just want it to end!"

Elise burst out into the night, leaving her father behind and Clint convincing him to let her have her moment alone. She didn't want a moment alone, she realized as she saw Karen and Sam beside the water and went the other way. She wanted a moment without fear, a moment with laughter, a moment with no bitterness. There was no place to go in this madness. No place where they weren't watched and stalked and threatened. No place without cops and guns and memories.

Clint caught up to her and swung her around to him. "Calm down, baby. Calm down!"

She jerked away from him, intent on heading for the boathouse where no one could watch her fall apart. Clint followed her into the musty structure and closed the door behind him. He flicked on the light, a dim yellow lantern attached to a beam on the ceiling, making the room into a graveyard of tall, deep shadows.

She set her foot on one of the boats docked there, bobbing with a calming rhythm that made her lower her voice. "I can't be calm anymore, Clint. I'm so angry. I've never been so angry." She turned around and leaned over a tackle box set on a table against the wall. "I feel used and manipulated and so scared right now. It's his fault, and I can't sit still and listen to how he did the honorable thing."

"What would you have done?" Clint's voice was stern, and Elise breathed a great sigh and pulled up onto the stool beside the table. The water made a lapping noise against the boats, and a soft breeze blew in from the open wall facing the water, ruffling her hair. Behind her was a workbench, covered with tools and fishing poles. Someone actually came here to find peace, she mused. "I'm asking you a question, Elise. What would you have done if you were the district attorney and your daughter's fiancé came to you with what I saw?"

"I don't know," she said quietly.

"That's too easy, babe. I want you to think about it. I want you to see that you would have done the same thing."

"I wouldn't have."

"Okay, let's see. Your daughter's fiancé comes to you and says he saw a politician commit murder. So you contact the police. Would you do that?"

"Yes, I suppose."

"All right. While you're handling things, the fiancé slips out and goes home, even though you told him to stay put. Next thing you know, someone's tried to kill him, and almost succeeded. What are your options? Would you try your damnedest to protect him?"

"Of course, but I wouldn't have to lie to my daughter to do it. And I wouldn't—"

"What if you knew that if your daughter knew

she'd be worried sick and would try to find him? What if you didn't want anyone to suspect that the fiancé was the witness, because you thought that was his best protection? And if the daughter knew why he'd really left, she'd insist on going with him? Would you deliberately want to set your own daughter up for that kind of danger?"

Elise dropped her face and covered it with a hand. "No."

"If your father had not done everything he could to protect me, I wouldn't have lived another day. I'm convinced of that."

Elise's head shot up. "You still might not, Clint! I'm convinced of that!"

Clint took her hands and made her look at him. "I will. As soon as we can, we'll go somewhere else and start over if you want to."

Elise dropped her head back and focused on a knot in the raw ceiling, letting her tears roll down her temples.

"And what will we do for work? We're good at what we do, Clint. We love it. There isn't anyplace else where we could do what we do and make such an impact. We've saved entire cities with our work. Are you telling me you don't mind just leaving all that behind and—"

"Damn it, Elise, if I've learned anything in the past eight months it's that you have to accept things. I don't want to leave my job. I didn't want to before. And I didn't want to leave you. But as long as I have you this time, I'll dig ditches for a living. I don't care."

Elise slid off the stool and into his secure embrace. He crushed her against him and buried his face in her hair. "I love you, Elise. There were days when I wanted to die, but I knew that you were still there, and somehow it all seemed worthwhile. I would dream of your eyes and the feel of your hair and the way you smell. Your dad kept me up to date on what you were doing, how you were coping. He brought me pictures of you. A few times, before you moved in with Karen, I even called you just to hear you say hello. Little things, but they kept me going. They kept me feeling, even when I sometimes just needed to be numb. I have you here now, and I'll do anything I can to keep it that way. Be happy, Elise. Please, be happy."

Elise lifted her face to his, all shiny and glowing in the yellow light of the lamp. "I am happy," she whispered. "I am." But mirrored in his eyes she saw her worry, her dread, and knew that he wasn't entirely resolved to its being the end either. "It's just that too many people have died. Gary, and Jake, and his brother. So many lives have been hurt. Neither one of us can ever be the same, and I miss that. I'd give anything if we could go back to being the people we used to be, where the worst worry in our minds was where to put the dikes and dams."

Clint kissed a mist-laden eyelid and brushed his fingers up through her hair. "We're the same people we always were, Elise. We didn't change to cope with this. We just had to dig a little deeper into ourselves than we ever did before. We'll be all right. If we survived this, we can survive anything." He pulled her toward the door and smiled down at her. "Let's go back and talk to your dad. I think it's time you forgave him. He's suffering too."

Elise heaved a great sigh. Not certain what she would do when she faced her father again, she wiped at her eyes and reached for the doorknob.

"Not so fast." A voice from the shadows beside the farther boat stopped them, and they both swung around. "Neither of you is going anywhere."

Clint's hand clamped protectively around Elise's, and he pushed her slowly behind him as he saw the glint of a gun in the man's hand. "Who are you?" he asked in a tremulous voice.

The man took another step forward, bringing his features partially into relief—the shaggy brown hair, the bitter set of dry lips, the bearded jaw. "I'm the man whose life you ruined," he whispered. "And I've come to repay the favor."

Elise felt a surge of nausea mingled with dizziness as she looked into the hard, aged eyes of the young man who had started this whole nightmare.

The dull, lifeless eyes of Jake Calloway.

CHAPTER SEVENTEEN

"I thought you were dead." Clint's voice was no more than a horrified whisper.

"I'm sure you wished it more than once," Jake said, keeping his voice low enough so that no one outside could hear.

"But they found your body."

Jake's frosty smile didn't reach his eyes. "It wasn't my body. It was Zeke's, the only guy I could trust. We were torching the building and leaving my fingerprints and clothes and stuff scattered around to make it look like I burned up there . . . ," he took a deep, shuddering breath, and months-old fatigue tugged at his features.

"You staged it? You killed someone to make us think you were dead?"

Rage and remembered terror broke through the dullness in Jake's eyes, giving him a mournful, yet youthful quality that took the edge off the cool sound of his voice. "Hell no, I didn't kill him! He was *helping* me! It was his freakin' idea! It's just that the fumes rose too fast, and he lit the fire too soon. I had already gotten out. We didn't know . . ." His voice fell off, and he hardened his expression and swallowed. "The fire back-lashed, and he was burned so bad that they couldn't even identify him. They found some of the stuff I left. Figured it was me."

Clint's nostrils flared in disgust. "Then you got what you wanted, after all."

The gun waved carelessly as Jake's haunted eyes glowered. "I never wanted him to die! We grew up together!" He swallowed back his emotion and his lips stretched like thin bands. "Anyway, don't give me that guilt crap, Jessup. I lost everything because of you. Where's *your* guilt?"

A flicker of pain passed over Clint's eyes, then vanished. "Oh, I had guilt, Jake. But it scarred over, just like my knife wound."

A deep-throated laugh rolled from Jake's throat. "You want to talk about scars, man? I have scars you can't even see, and they all date back to that night."

Elise was trembling, but Clint's hands were steady as they held her behind him, telling her not to panic, telling her to trust him. "It could have gone the other way. I saw you as a mixed-up kid who'd gotten in over his head. A jury proba-bly would have seen the same thing, until you tried to shut me up."

"It never would have gone to a jury," Jake snapped, shaking his head adamantly. "I'd have been dead before they had even set a court date. All it would have taken was for Givanti to know I'd screwed up."

"Well, he did find out and you're still here, aren't you?"

Jake steadied his gun, though his hands trembled over it. "Only because he didn't know about it until you came to court. You might say I've kept a low profile the last few months. No one knew except my brother and Zeke."

"Your . . . your brother?" Elise's hoarse exclamation came unbidden. Jake's utterance of it suddenly made the death so much more tragic.

"Yeah, my brother." Jake's lips quivered, and his eyes misted, though he blinked to cover the crack in his hard shell. He swallowed and lowered his gun distractedly. "And you got him too." He looked at the ceiling and raked his free hand through his unkempt hair. "He should have killed you, instead of the other way around. And I should have killed you in that ambulance, instead of Rivers. But nothing went right!" He caught himself, and wiped back the moisture blurring his eyes. "Ironic that Rivers was the only one of you I didn't want. He wasn't even supposed to be there. He was supposed to be here."

It took a moment for Jake's words to penetrate, but when they did, Clint's face drained of all its color.

"What?" Clint's question came on an astonished whisper.

Jake nodded his head and slumped his shoulders. "That's right. How do you think I found out where you were? How do you think I knew that you'd be in ambulances going down I-20, or

264

that you were hiding here? If you'd done everything the way he said you were going to, you'd be dead now."

Clint clutched Elise's hand, trying to steady himself against the sudden dawning of cold betrayal. "He helped you?"

"Just to the point of telling me where you could be found. He didn't know what I was gonna do, but I doubt if he cared much. I made my intentions pretty clear."

Clint's face was white, and his dark eyes focused on the shadows. "That's why he got out of the car. He thought if you saw that he was there you'd wait."

"I couldn't wait!" Jake said through his teeth. "I'd waited for eight months."

Fear slipped as shock seeped in, and Elise's wide blue eyes filled with fresh horror. "Why would Gary help you?" she asked raggedly. "Why?"

"Revenge," Jake said simply, as if it was the most logical emotion in the world. "He hated Clint. He wouldn't have killed him himself. He was too yellow. But he did everything he could to make sure that I did. He had a condition, though. He wanted Elise left unharmed."

"She wouldn't have been if your brother's attempt hadn't failed. She would have been killed with me!" Clint said.

"So Rivers said." He wiped at the perspiration on his brow with the back of the hand holding the gun. "And I told him that if he wanted her alive, he'd have to protect her himself. I didn't have time to be all that discriminating when my chance came."

Clint's nails bit into the palms of his hands, and power borne of rage coiled up inside of him, waiting for the moment to vent itself.

"And I tried," Jake went on. "I should have killed you when you went back to Vicksburg, thinking I was dead. I should have blown you away then."

"You? You were the one following Elise? You sent her that letter?"

"Surprised?" Jake tried to look satisfied, but his expression fell far short. "And I was the one following her, the one your friend managed to lose, until I made contact with Rivers and talked him into helping me. And you thought it was a whole freakin' crime ring, didn't you? That Givanti's power reached everywhere. But I was the only one who wanted you dead. I was the only one who came after you." He sneered and nodded toward the water, as if Givanti were standing there. "His little group of wimps even took off the minute the verdict came in. Scattered all over, in case they were next. You think any of them cared anything about revenge? They were too worried about saving their hides. I'm the only one who had anything to gain by watching them bury you."

"Like what?" Clint asked. Jake was inching toward them, his gun rising to eye level. "Will it change anything? Haven't we all been through enough hell?"

"You don't know what hell is. But you're about to, old pal. You're about to find out."

Clint stiffened, every muscle in his body rigid. Elise's backbone straightened as well, and she held her breath in defiance of that gun. His fingers bit into her skin when she tried to push around him, desperate to protect the man she loved as he had protected her.

"If you pull that trigger," Clint said, "you won't live to see me hit the ground. I don't have to tell you what kind of security I have out there."

"It would be worth it," Jake said. His eyes glittered under the feeble light, making what he was about to do seem less cruel, less cold. "But it won't happen that way. I got in here before you even got back today, and I'll get out. I'm a good swimmer. I'll be long gone before they get through the door."

He cocked the pistol and took another step closer.

"Don't!" Elise jerked free of Clint and stepped around him. "Jake, don't! Please!"

"Get out of my way, Elise," Jake said. "I have nothing against you, but I'll blow you away if you don't move."

Clint's breath was audible now, and his eyes locked with Jake's as if holding his gaze could make him drop his intention. "Elise, move!" Clint's voice was quietly controlled, but she didn't heed his order. Somehow, she was going to stop this madness, and her only bet was that Jake couldn't shoot her as easily as he could Clint.

"Move, damn it!" Jake's arm lashed out and grabbed her wrist. She gasped as he jerked her against him and clamped his free arm over her throat, but the gun remained pointed at Clint's head.

Clint's face went white, and a band of perspiration glistened on his forehead. "Jake, let her go," he whispered. "Let her go, and you can do whatever you want with me. You don't need her."

"She could be my ticket out of here," Jake said, his eyes dancing at the idea. "With her, I won't have to swim a couple of miles. I could walk right through those jackasses who think they've protected you so well. Hell, the DA's daughter could do miracles for me. I could get so far out of here they'd never find me."

Clint swallowed, and a muscle on his temple twitched. He raised his palms slowly, as if to calm a rabid, foaming beast. "Don't do it, Jake. This is between you and me. You could dive into that water and swim away right now, and no one would ever know you'd been here. You could even take one of the boats. I'd cover for you."

"You think I'm a moron?" Jake's arm clamped tighter around Elise's throat, inhibiting her breath, and she closed her eyes. "I didn't come here to talk to you. I came here to watch you bleed. I came here to see you die."

Elise tried to find her voice. "Jake . . ."

His arm tightened so hard around her throat that a wave of dizziness splashed over her. The veins in her neck battled against the arm acting as a tourniquet, but all she saw was the barrel of that pistol as Jake leveled it between Clint's eyes, and the knuckle of his finger turning white as it began to close over the trigger.

Sam pulled away from Karen and turned toward the boathouse, furrowed lines shading his eyes.

"What's the matter?" she asked.

"They've been in there too long," he said. "I don't like it."

"They're okay. Don't worry so much."

He took a few steps toward the boathouse, then looked back at Karen. "Weren't they fighting?"

"Sounded like it when they went in there."

"Then why is it so quiet now?"

Karen smiled and shrugged her brows. "Maybe they made up. Or killed each other."

Sam didn't acknowledge the reference to their joke the first night they were together. "I'm going to check," Sam said, starting toward the boathouse.

Karen grabbed his arm and stopped him with a wink. "I wouldn't do that if I were you. You might interrupt something. Now why don't you try to get your mind off work?"

"My mind is never entirely off work." He wrenched his eyes from the boathouse and threw up his hands. "Ah, you're probably right. I've gotten too paranoid. The place is crawling with cops. What could possibly happen in there?"

"Just a little romance," she said with utmost confidence. "And absolutely nothing else."

* * *

Clint's eyes locked unyieldingly with Jake's as the cold barrel of the Saturday night special touched his forehead. "It won't solve anything, Jake," he whispered.

"It'll solve everything."

"For a minute, maybe. But it won't bring your brother or your friend back. Your brother wouldn't even be dead if he hadn't tried to kill me. I cared about you, Jake. That was my worst mistake. I thought I could help you."

"Help me?" Jake gave a dry, brittle laugh. "Get off the self-righteous act. Man, you loved it. You stumbled on something way above your mundane world, and you saw it as a chance for a cheap thrill."

"You think I put my life on hold for a cheap thrill?" Clint uttered in disgust. "Is that why you got involved?"

Jake looked at the water, rippling in the distance with mocking peace that would never be his again. "Man, I didn't have an old man to put me through college, or a genius IQ that got me scholarships. I found ways to do pretty well, but you disapproved, so you shot it all down. And you're going to pay." The words were uttered matter-of-factly, as if their events had come to a logical, inflexible end.

Clint disregarded the gun and looked into the pained depths of his enemy's pale eyes. "Don't give me the poor kid routine. I've been there, pal. If anybody knows about struggle, I do. Nobody helped me, either. But you knew you could have come to me when things got bad."

"Oh, come off it, man. Elise was your free ride. Her old man had so much money, you'd never have to hurt again. You were so wrapped up in that fairy-tale wedding of yours, you wouldn't have given my problems a second thought."

"Obviously I did," Clint ground out through stiff lips. "Look what it cost me."

"Your life, man!" Jake said, clamping his arm tighter around Elise's neck. "And your lady, and everything you ever cared about. Say your prayers, man! This'll be your last chance."

His knuckle was turning white again, about to squeeze the trigger, and something inside Elise snapped. Clamping her hands together, she summoned all her might and swung her arms up, knocking Jake's stiff aim skyward.

Instantly, Clint's hands clamped over Jake's wrist, wrestling for the gun above their heads, and Jake lost his hold on Elise. A cry tore from her throat as strength foiled intention, and she scrambled for the door in horror when she saw both hands clamped over the pistol, muscles straining, cords throbbing, fingers clawing. The gun was descending, regaining its aim on Clint, pointing just over his shoulder, turning toward his head . . .

She heard herself scream, and as if in slow motion, she turned back and started toward them in a desperate attempt to stop them.

But suddenly the gun went off, and she was hurled back against the wall in a blinding burst of

pain, and she heard Clint scream, "Eli-i-i-ise!"
And she felt herself falling . . . falling . . .
falling into an abyss of herself, until there was
nothing left but blackness and the cruel, cold
chill of loss.

CHAPTER EIGHTEEN

"Eli-i-i-se!" Clint's voice rang out like death, skipping over the water and reaching the ears of everyone within a mile. Elise lay motionless on the floor, a widening ring of blood painting her arm.

The door burst open, and Sam shouted, "Police! Freeze!"

The gun suddenly came free of Jake's hand. Clutching it in a shaking hand, Clint grabbed the man's collar and slammed him against the wall, the pistol shaking in his hand. "You bastard! I'll kill you!"

"Cl . . . Clint?" Elise's weak voice came like the answer to a prayer, melting his immediate intent. She was not dead. Oh thank God, she was not dead.

He dropped Jake to his knees and rushed to her just as Sam stepped inside, his gun in his hand, the others at his heels. Scooping her up in his arms, he held her helplessy.

Eric Cranston barreled in and fell to his knees

beside his daughter. "Oh, my God! We've got to get her to a hospital!"

Clint nodded blindly. "Take her. Hurry!"

With the help of another officer, Cranston pried Clint's arms loose and gathered her into his arms. When they had darted out of the boat-house, Clint stood up and stalked over to Jake, who knelt in a shiver at the guns trained on him. "Get up, you bastard!" he gritted, holding his gun to the man's temple. "Get up and look death in the eye!"

Jake gulped audibly, and stood up, trembling. "You can't shoot me. I'm unarmed, and there are too many witnesses."

Clint's eyes were as dark as death. He cocked the pistol.

"Don't do it, Clint!" Sam's plea came slowly, cautiously. "Don't let it end this way. Let us take him in."

"You'll take him in in a hearse," Clint promised. He pressed the gun harder against Jake's head.

"Clint, you're not a killer. Don't do it!"

Clint struggled with the emotion throbbing in his head. "You've killed before. I can do it too."

"You're not me, Clint. You won't be able to live with it! It's over! All you have to do is drop the gun! Damn it, Clint, drop the gun!"

"I . . . can't." Perspiration dripped from his brow and burned his eyes, and Jake squeezed his eyes shut. He was a kid, still a kid, as mean and vicious as the most hardened criminal. And as scared as a boy faced with a mad dog. He looked at that boy and saw through the hatred and re-called the first day he had met him. He had been in such awe of the work the corps of engineers were doing there. He'd even seemed in awe of Clint himself. What had happened to him?

Oh, the hate. It gnawed at Clint's stomach like an acid burning its way out. He wanted to pull the trigger. He wanted to hurt him the way he had hurt Elise.

But then what? Would Clint ever be the same, after having killed a man? Would he be able to go on with life as if the past eight months had just been an interlude that was now behind him? Or would it go with him for the rest of his life? Once he crossed that threshold of revenge, he was no better than Jake. Jake had already cost him too much. He would not give him his soul for a cold trophy called revenge.

Slowly, as if it took every ounce of strength he had left, Clint dropped the gun to his side and stepped out of Sam's way.

Sam dashed forward, but before he reached him, Jake dove between the two boats and began to swim underwater. Suddenly, Sam fell to one knee and opened fire.

Someone drove the eighteen-wheeler to the bank, shining its headlights over the rippling sur-face of the reservoir. And finally they saw Jake, the life gone out of his body.

Clint only stared dully at him as some of the men waded out to bring him back. Jake Calloway was really dead, but somehow the knowledge didn't hold much joy.

Turning his back on the sight, Clint ran back toward the house to find what they had done with Elise. "Where is she?"

"In the car," Karen cried. "They're about to take her to the—"

Clint didn't hear the rest. The car was turning around on the grass, about to leave, and Clint dashed after it. "Stop! I'm coming with you!"

The car stopped, and Clint got in. Cranston was holding Elise in the backseat, and Clint leaned over her as the car lurched forward. "Elise?" His voice was on the edge of tears, and Elise opened her eyes.

"Is it over?" she whispered.

He took her hand. "Yes, baby. It's over. It's all over."

Elise closed her eyes again.

"We'll be all right," Clint said hoarsely, pushing her hair back from her face. "We'll be all right now."

An hour later, Clint sat helplessly in the hospital waiting room, staring at the wall, waiting to hear yet another verdict that would determine the course of the rest of his life. Would Elise die? Would that be the tragic ending to this absurd production his life had become?

He closed his eyes and thought back to the day he had chased her in his Bronco and run her off the road. Why had he done that? Why hadn't he just left things alone, until he was safe? Why hadn't he been more patient? Why hadn't he known that Jake wasn't really dead? If he'd just left her alone, he wouldn't have had to bring her with him. And her life would never have been in danger.

He searched the farthest corners of his mind and tried to find some clue that she would be all right. She had not completely lost consciousness all the way to the hospital. Maybe that was good. And she had spoken. And just before they wheeled her away in the emergency room, she had smiled at him. He leaned forward and cupped his face in his hands. Oh God, did he dare hope that she would be all right? He looked over his fingertips to the door where they had taken her. If only they had let him stay with her. If only he could be there . . .

The door swung open, and the emergency room doctor came out. Clint, Karen, Sam, and Elise's father all stood at the same time, none of them asking anything for fear the answer was not what they wanted to hear.

"She's going to be fine," the doctor said. "The bullet didn't even touch the bone. She also has a slight concussion from hitting her head when she fell. Besides some pretty fierce pain, she's going to be completely well soon. We'd like to keep her for a couple of days for observation, though."

Clint sank onto the vinyl sofa, a sudden surge of emotion racking his body. Covering his face, he sent up a silent prayer of thanks, while the others around him expressed relief in their own ways. She was okay. She was fine. She was safe.

"She wants to see Mr. Jessup," the doctor said.

"We've got her on some pain medication, but she's pretty alert."

Clint stood up again. "Can I stay here with her tonight? I don't want to leave her."

"I don't think she'd let you go if you wanted to," the doctor said with a smile. "Come on. I'll take you to her."

Sam laced his fingers through Karen's hand as he pulled her with him across the hospital parking lot, lit only by yellow circles of light from street lamps overhead. He had been quiet since the incident at the reservoir, and now that Elise was fine, that had not changed.

"Guess it's all over," Karen said quietly when they reached his car.

"Yeah. Over."

He leaned against the car and looked up into the sky. She followed his eyes and wondered what he saw.

"What's the matter?"

"Nothing."

The dead end hurt her. Was the tiny bit of progress they'd made toward a relationship going to fizzle out just like that? She looked down at the grimy pavement beneath her feet and frowned. She guessed it was.

Ironic, she thought. All this time she had been afraid of Sam's getting killed or wounded. She'd almost expected to lose him that way, now that she'd found him. She hadn't counted on losing him to indifference.

Clearing her throat, she turned toward him. "I

think I'll go on back in. Maybe they'll let me see Elise."

Sam nodded, as if he didn't care.

Lifting her chin with mendacious strength, Karen started to walk away.

"Karen?" Sam's voice was soft, reluctant, when it stopped her. Slowly, she turned around, bracing herself for an explanation about how it had been nice while it lasted. His eyes were so sad that they wrung her heart and forced her to forgive him even before he sent her on her way. "I don't deserve to have you stay," he whispered, "but I don't want you to go."

His voice teetered on the edge of emotion, and she went back to him, hands jammed in her pockets, heart jamming her throat. "What do you mean you don't deserve it?"

He sighed deeply, and reached for her hand. "I mean that I've been such a failure throughout this whole thing."

"A what?" She took his other hand and gazed at him with disbelief in her expression. "How can you say that? We're alive. We came out of it."

"Not because of anything I did. In fact, if I'd done my job, Elise wouldn't be up in that hospital bed right now."

"No," Karen agreed. "If you'd done things differently, she'd be dead. And so would Clint. In fact, they would have died in that barn when it exploded the other day."

"One accomplishment does not erase failure," he said, his eyes full of anguish. "I'm a cop. I

279

shouldn't have let them go into that boathouse alone. I should have suspected . . ."

"You and the other twenty cops on the grounds thought it was all right. Are you saying that it's okay for them to make a miscalculation, but it isn't for you?"

"I was Clint's friend. I was his guard. And until today I was a better cop than those other guys."

"Until me," she said as the real problem became clear to her.

"What?" The question was meant to be innocent, but she sensed that she had hit a nerve. She knew he saw his feelings for her as a new weakness that interfered, and she resented it.

"It all boils down to me. If I hadn't stopped you, you would have gone into the boathouse. If you hadn't been with me, you might never have let them go in."

Sam was silent for a moment, then he dropped her hand. "I shouldn't have let my attention be so divided when I was on duty. It almost cost Clint and Elise their lives."

"And since you're virtually always on duty," she said in a despairing, sullen voice, "I guess that means it's impossible for you to have any kind of relationship. Is that what you're saying?"

"No," he whispered. "I don't think that's what I'm saying."

"Wait a minute. Let me try again," she said, her voice growing louder. "You think you deserve to be punished for not being psychic and not getting to Jake Calloway before he got to Clint and

Elise. So your punishment is to go through life alone, nipping good possibilities for relationships in the bud, is that it?"

"No," he said, swallowing. "I'm not looking for punishment."

"Then what are you looking for?" she snapped furiously. Her eyes were misting over, and his hand came up to stroke her face.

Suddenly, he smiled. "Someone to tell me it's okay," he whispered. "Someone to hold me and give me focus and tell me I didn't screw up as bad as I think I did."

Karen inclined her head helplessly, and her shoulders slumped in relief. "You've got it," she whispered. She slid her arms around his waist, and he pulled her tightly against him.

"I think what I was trying to say," he whispered against her hair, "is that since I can't really divide my attentions between romance and work, maybe it's time for me to make a change. Maybe it's time for me to choose."

Karen felt him slipping away again, and she clung tighter. "I never put much faith in guarantees," she assured him, almost desperately. "I don't need them. Please don't choose between us. I can live with your job."

Sam framed her face and pressed his forehead against hers. "You crazy little thing. You think I wouldn't choose you, don't you?"

Tears spilled over Karen's lashes, and she closed her eyes. "You don't have to choose," she whispered again.

"Yes, I do," he whispered. "Because suddenly staying alive seems pretty important to me."

His kiss was like molten joy poured over raw nerves, coaxing her to accept the choice he had already made, coaxing her to believe that he was offering guarantees, coaxing her to rejoice in the sacrifice that resulted in so much reward.

And suddenly being alive seemed wondrously precious to Karen.

Clint sat on the hospital bed next to Elise, cradling her against him. They'd have to do surgery if they expected to separate them, he told himself. Because he had no intentions of ever leaving her side again.

The door opened, and Eric Cranston stepped into the softly lit room. Elise sat up and gave him an unsteady smile. "Hi, Dad."

With eyes as humble and frightened as she had ever seen them, he entered the room. He was a handsome man, she thought for the first time. It was no wonder that her mother had adored him. Or that Elise had always been able to forgive him.

"How do you feel?" he asked.

"I'm fine, Dad. How are you?"

"A little shaken," he admitted. Awkwardly, he pulled up a chair to the bedside and sat down, leaning forward. "I thought I'd lost you." He covered his face and shook his head. "I would never have forgiven myself."

Elise sat up, and Clint started to get off of the bed. "I'll step outside and—"

"No," Eric Cranston said. "Stay. You're part

of this family, and you belong here. Besides, I owe you a fierce apology."

"No." Clint held up a hand to stem the regrets. "I did all this for my conscience, not because you—"

"I'm not apologizing for that," Cranston cut in softly. "I'm apologizing for undermining you by sending Gary Rivers to protect Elise. At the time it seemed as if someone who cared for her would do a better job. It was stupid, and it must have made things so much harder on you. And it turned out to be such a disaster."

Clint looked down at Elise's palm and stroked his hand across it. "I'll admit I cursed you for that a few times."

"You should have." Cranston rubbed at his pleated forehead, and shook his head. "I misjudged him terribly. I never suspected—"

Clint reached across Elise and touched the older man's shoulder. "Enough said. It's over, and I think I can understand your reasoning. No hard feelings."

Cranston released a heavy breath, then looked at his daughter. "And now, my apology to you," he said.

Elise shook her head. She wouldn't withhold her forgiveness or her love. She didn't want her father to be more miserable than he must have been for the past few months, fearing for her life and for Clint's. Now she knew those fears had been valid, and his decisions sound. She had been in danger, and the outcome could have been much worse. "Dad, I'm sorry I was so upset before. I needed someone to blame, and you were there." Her eyes misted over, and she looked at the ceiling. "It was the lie that really hurt. I didn't understand it."

Cranston issued a rasping sigh. "I probably could have handled it better. But I was so desperate to protect you. You were all I had left. Can't you see that?"

Elise nodded mutely.

Cranston sat back in his chair and looked out the window, at the black clouds roiling in front of the moon and the rain just beginning to sprinkle against the hospital panes. "When your mother died, I thought my whole world would crumble. I thought there was nothing left. But there was. There was a little girl with big blue, trusting eyes, eyes that said, 'the world is good.' Eyes that didn't understand death and pain and grief. Eyes that had the power to heal." He wiped his own eyes and went on. "And I didn't want you to understand those things. I wanted you to go on believing in the power of love and the power of life. And I just didn't have the strength to tell you that your mother had died. I tried. I really did. But the most I could get out was that she had gone away, and you would look at me with those confused eyes and give me a hundred reasons why you knew she would be back. I just couldn't make myself give you the one reason why she wouldn't. Because, in a way, I guess I could almost believe she'd be back myself, if you believed it." He wiped at his eyes, and brought his gaze back to his daughter.

Elise caught her breath and wiped at the tears blurring her eyes. "Oh, Daddy," she whispered.

He nodded. "It was wrong and selfish, but it was all I could do at the time. Just like lying to you about Clint was all I knew to do. And every time I looked in your eyes after he left, it was like a knife being twisted inside me. You were so hurt, but I believed that was better than letting you risk your life going after him. And you know that's what you would have done."

She swallowed. "Yes."

He stood up and sat on the bed, facing her and Clint. "I love you, honey. I need you to forgive me."

"There's nothing to forgive," she whispered. "We each handled that nightmare in our own way. It's over now."

Her father reached across the bed with an embrace that included Clint. "As soon as I leave here, I'm going for the minister. We have a wedding to plan, and there's no time to waste."

Elise breathed an enormous sigh and smiled at Clint. "Just give me a license and a ring and a few months of uninterrupted peace with the man I love. And then I'll be back to myself."

"Is that possible?" Clint asked softly. "Will any of us ever be ourselves again?"

"No," Cranston said. "We've all changed. But we're stronger now. None of us will ever take the people we love or the time we have with them for granted again."

Clint's arms tightened around Elise, reaffirming that strength that filtered into their love, promising never to be torn asunder, never to be mistrusted, never to turn against them again.

In the throes of sleep later that night, Elise struggled with the colliding images ranting through her mind like faces in a haunted house. Jake's face and the cold, cruel glint of his gun; the dead boy on the bluff; the fire that had been meant to consume her and Clint; the navy hooded jackets; the pain of betrayal that was not really betrayal. But on the heels of the horror came an unyielding Bronco to chase her down and rescue her from her grief. And the horror was gone.

She opened her eyes and Clint smiled down at her. It wasn't all a dream. He was here, and no matter what had transpired before this moment, she was in his arms now.

"I love you, Clint," she whispered.

"I love you too, baby," he said, pulling her closer against him. "Go back to sleep."

"You won't leave?"

"Not until you push me away," he said.

"Then you'll be here a long time, Superman."

"That's my plan," Clint said with a smile as he rolled over to kiss her. "That's been my plan all along."

And, finally, Elise knew that faith that she had abandoned so long ago. No longer would it be a flimsy piece of self-betrayal. It would become the backbone of her secure world. A world she had fought for and won. The cornerstone of their little square of paradise.